Scares & Dares

A Paranormal Witch Cozy Witch Mystery

Book Store Cozy Mystery Series
Book 4

Lucinda Race

MC Two Press

Copyright © 2023 Lucinda Race

Editor Kimberly Dawn
Cover design by Mariah Sinclair

Manufactured in the United States of America
First Edition October 2023

Print Edition ISBN 978-1-954520-51-6
E-book ISBN 978-1-954520-50-9

Author's Note

Hi and welcome to my world of cozy mystery.

I hope you love my characters as much as I do. So, turn the page and happy sleuthing. If you'd like to stay in touch, please join my Newsletter. I release it twice per month with tidbits, recipes and an occasional special gift just for my readers so sign up here:
https:// lucindarace.com/newsletter/
and there's a free cozy mystery when you join!

Happy reading...

**Special note to my readers: My books are drawn entirely from my brain. AI was not used in the creation or editing of this book.

Pembroke Cove, ME

1. Robin's Cafe
2. Bygone Antiques
3. The Pembroke Cliffs
4. Cozy Nook Bookstore
5. Twisted Scissors Hair Salon
6. Betty's Market
7. Old Town Libary
8. Miss Judy's Dance Studio
9. The Sweet Spot Baker
10. Bee Bee's Boutique
11. Tuckers Hardware Store
12. The Copper Kettle
13. Police Station
14. Town Hall

Chapter 1
Lily

QUICK NOTE: If you enjoy Scares & Dares, be sure to check out my offer for a FREE bonus at the end. With that, happy reading!

* * *

"Halloween is four days away." Pointing at the calendar on the wall, I looked at my boyfriend, Gage; my best friend, Nikki; and her guy, Steve, who were relaxing around my kitchen table. We were done stuffing our faces with meat lovers and extra-cheese pizza. "I know it's late in the game, but we've been tasked with taking over decorating and running the haunted house on All Hallows Eve. But if we're going to be successful, we have to come up with a foolproof plan. Everyone in Pembroke Cove expects to be scared out of their boots after dark. So, we need to have two versions, one for the kiddos and an adult-orientated theme."

Gage ran his finger around the edge of his glass. "That

doesn't give us much time to bring in volunteers and build the sets. I can reach out to Corbin Marks, and maybe with a little help from our favorite witches, my mom and your Aunt Mimi, along with you ladies, we can get it done in time."

My familiar, Milo, stalked into the room and looked at the two dogs—Brutus, a great Dane Gage had adopted and Murphy, Nikki's retriever—snoozing in front of the door. "My dear witch," he grumbled good-naturedly, "you should have told me we were having guests. It appears I've snoozed through most of the fun if the sleeping dogs are any indication of what happened in here."

Over the last few months, I had gotten used to my cat talking to me and the only person in the room who could hear him besides me was Nikki. Both Gage and Steve were non-magical and what they heard was Milo meowing whenever he spoke. I scooped him off the floor and held him close to my chest, nuzzling his head. "We're planning the haunted house. Any good ideas?"

"Now, why would I have any thoughts on that subject. I don't like anything that is scary. Humans are looking to get spooked when they don't even realize right in their own backyards are witches, wizards, and a few other paranormal creatures."

I gently turned his head to look at me. "Wait? What did you say?"

Milo tapped my cheek with his soft paw. "Put me down on the floor. I have things to do and if you would read more of your book, *Practical Beginnings*, you'd know all that our small town has to offer." He did little to keep the frustration from his voice.

Before I did as he asked, I had to know, "What do you mean others?"

"That's for me to know and you to find out." He wriggled out of my hands and slinked from the room without a backward glance.

Gage gestured to Milo's retreating form. "What was that all about?"

"My familiar just informed me there are other paranormal beings living in Pembroke Cove and not just witches and wizards." I gave Nikki a sharp look. "Did you know this?"

She shrugged but didn't look at me. "It's no big deal and nothing to worry about. Most of the time it's just witches and the occasional wizard hanging out, and if anyone does come around, it's in the spring."

With her noncommittal response, I figured it was a topic of conversation left for another day, especially if we had five or six months before anyone showed up. But what kind of paranormals could there be? Maybe my book, *Practical Beginnings*, would shed some light on the topic. And when the guys weren't around, I could get Nikki to open up.

"Alright then, let's talk about what we can use from last year." I got up and grabbed my laptop from the counter and sat back down. "I talked to Alice and Bea who were both on the committee last year, and Bea sent me some pictures of what they stored in the shed behind the animal shelter." I tapped a few keys and turned the screen so my friends could see it. "We're going to hold it at the grange hall like it's been in past years, but I'm hoping we can have a hay bale walkway and place some skeletons around with spooky music and cobwebs. In the entrance we could have a mural that looks like an old mansion with ripped wallpaper that has fallen into disrepair or something." My ideas were starting to flow so I kept going. "Then we can have areas with different scenes; some will have people as props, like the table with the domed platter and when the dome comes off, it's just a talking head. It goes without saying spooky music and spiderwebs are everywhere inside. Then I'll ask if Aunt Mimi could have a witch area with a cauldron, stirring up potions, and Nate could be her ghoul."

Nikki grinned. "They'll jump at the chance."

I nodded. "I'd like to have a couple of vampires popping out of coffins, a mummy or two that's animated or real, and maybe some people in armor that move around to scare folks."

Gage rubbed his hands together. "A magic mirror and crystal ball are both good options. My mom would be happy to help."

My enthusiasm seemed to be contagious.

Steve said, "What about doors opening and closing and candles everywhere?"

"Battery operated," Gage interjected. "We don't want to have to call the fire company. If we don't get enough volunteers, the animated props can fill in where we don't have live bodies."

"There should be jack-o'-lanterns everywhere. I'll bet Marshall Stone will donate to the cause and maybe he'll even help carve." Nikki sighed. "I love carving faces."

"I'm sure with your kitchen witch abilities, they're a work of art." I snapped my fingers as my gaze slid to my witchcraft book. "We need a fake spell book that opens and closes on its own; Aunt Mimi can cast a spell for that. Maybe with a funny, but fake incantation on the page in case someone reads it."

Nodding, Gage said, "Some well-placed lifelike rats and other critters that move, covered with glow-in-the-dark paint. And I'll even buy some roses for my girl and she can let them die before using them at the entrance of the haunted house."

I could feel the frown form on my face. Thinking of our most recent death in town where a local rose grower had been killed and I used this board to jot down clues and suspects two other times. But I didn't say anything to cause anyone to go down that sad path. "I think we have a lot of good ideas. Let's write them down and see who we can line up to donate or volunteer to help."

Gage went to the pantry closet and pulled out my clue chalkboard. A chill raced over my arms when my mind drifted to the three murders in town. This time the board would be used for a happy occasion and that would kick the bad vibes right to the curb.

"Good idea. We can take pictures on our phone so if you find something that will work, text me and I'll add the information to our master list." I took the chalk from Gage's fingers and jotted down all the ideas we had come up with.

Nikki surveyed the list and smiled. "This is a good start. Now let's see about getting people to help. Like Lily said, we don't have a lot of time to make this happen and I want to do all we can to give this town the most memorable haunted house ever."

I flashed Gage an inquiring look. "Do you think Dax will help out since his investigation seems to have gone cold?" Dax Peters was the most recent, temporary transplant to our small town. He was a big city federal investigator on the trail of a real estate scheme that had infiltrated and had, in some ways, been responsible for two people dying in Pembroke Cove. The head librarian had been forcing people, who had secrets to hide, to pay bribes, and then a real estate agent was swindling people out of profits from selling their homes. All for hefty kickbacks from an unknown Mr. Big. Squaring my shoulders, I pushed all of those worries aside. We had fun to focus on and lots of it. The kids both young and old alike were looking forward to the haunted house.

Gage tapped out a text on his phone and it quickly pinged with an incoming message. He grinned. "Dax loves Halloween and he'd love to help. Should I ask him to come over?"

I looked at our tiny committee of three plus me. "The more the merrier but see if he'll swing by The Sweet Spot and pick up a box of pastries if they're still open. I'll make coffee."

Nikki smiled. "If I had known your sweet tooth was kicking in and you wanted dessert, I would have baked."

Glancing at the wall clock, I said, "On second thought, just tell him to come on over. William will be closed by now."

With a quick nod, Gage set his phone aside. "Dax should be here in about fifteen minutes."

"Has he finally moved out of the motel?" Steve asked.

"Not yet, but last week, when he stopped in the bookstore, I asked him if he was thinking about making our little cove a permanent home, but he's still on the fence. I'm sure it's hard to uproot your life and move from a place where you live anonymously to a place where everyone knows when you sneeze."

Gage raised an eyebrow as if asking me to expand on my conversation with Dax. I shrugged and said, "It was no big deal. With no leads to follow up on, he's been reading a lot more."

"There is a library," Gage grumbled and I had to smile.

"Green has never been your color." I dropped a kiss on his cheek before getting up to start the coffee.

Nikki joined me. "I'll rustle up something sweet."

Steve leaned back in his chair and grinned. "Sometimes it's great being engaged to a witch."

I dropped the glass carafe in the sink and didn't care if it broke. "You're engaged? Why didn't you tell me?"

"Steve and I decided we'd work it into the conversation. It just happened this morning when I was up to my elbows in pie crust. It was so romantic." A dreamy look floated over her face and she withdrew a stunning diamond ring from her jeans pocket and slipped it on her finger before placing her left hand over her heart. "Isn't it beautiful?"

Gage got up and hugged Nikki and then vigorously shook Steve's hand. "Congratulations. You're one lucky guy."

"Don't I know it." He wiggled his eyebrows and said, "Jump in; the water's like a hot tub in winter."

I couldn't help but snort. "It took us fifteen years after we graduated college to go on our first date just a couple of weeks ago. We are *so* not ready to jump in and get engaged."

Nikki gave me a long look. "You and Gage have been better friends than most married couples I know, and that is the basis of a good marriage. Look at me and Steve. It took us a long time to let our friendship develop into love and now we're getting married." She grabbed my hands. "Please tell me you'll be my maid of honor?"

Throwing my arms around her, I held her close. "Just try and stop me."

Steve said, "Gage. Any chance you'd stand up for me?"

Gage clapped him on the shoulder. "No place I'd rather be."

Nikki giggled. "We haven't set the date yet but probably spring or summer."

Steve said, "Or sooner if I can convince my future wife to agree."

I overlooked that comment. "Like around the time when we might get paranormal company?" I hoped my question would prompt a response.

She clasped my hand. "Stop worrying about what may or might not happen. We should all have dinner on Friday and start talking about our wedding plans."

I looked at Gage, and he said, "I'm free."

Taking his hand and grinning at Nikki and Steve, I said, "Then we have our first official wedding planning night."

A knock at the door stopped the conversation and with a flick of her wrist, Nikki had a pumpkin cheesecake sitting on the counter. She gave me one of those smiles when she wasn't trying to show off how strong her magic was and mine wasn't. "It's no big deal; I just summoned it from my house to yours."

Gage opened the door for Dax.

He held up a hand in greeting. In his soft Southern drawl, he said, "Hey, everyone. Thanks for including me. Halloween is my favorite holiday." He spotted the cheesecake on the counter and grinned. "Just in time for dessert too."

I glanced at the sink and was relieved to see the carafe was in one piece after dropping it. "Come in. I was just making coffee and we can firm up plans for the big event."

He pulled up a chair and sat down at the table, then noticed the open laptop. Glancing at this list, he said, "Impressive. But is there enough time to get this all done and ready in three days? You can't count the day it opens to still be constructing the scenes. Then it's all about the finishing touches."

Gage grinned. "You have no idea what these ladies can

do when they put their minds to it and we have a list of volunteers to help too. Mine and Lily's parents will pitch in as well as her aunt and Nate."

Nikki said, "My parents don't live in Pembroke Cove anymore, but Steve's family will help."

Steve took her hand and grinned. "Yeah, especially after we tell them our news. Everyone is going to want to be around."

Dax looked around our group. "News?"

"I popped the question to my lovely Nikki and she said yes."

I swear if Steve were a witch, he'd be floating, and I knew that was possible based on what I had read in my book.

"That's great. Congratulations to both of you." His smile was wide, but there was a bit of sadness lingering in his eyes. Could it be he was still feeling like he was on the outside looking in? Hopefully working on this event would change all that.

With the coffee pot turned on, I sat in the chair next to Gage. "Dax, tell us, do you want to be in a scene or just behind them?"

He sat up straight in the chair and grinned. "Are you kidding? I want to be a vampire lying in a coffin."

I couldn't help but shudder. There was something about the lore of vampires and vampire-themed movies that set my teeth on edge. I mustered up enthusiasm to say, "That's one way to scare people coming through, but only after we finish with the kiddos. I don't want to give a youngster the fright of their lives."

Chapter 2
Lily

Over the next three days, everyone who agreed to help with the haunted house was working like a whirling dervish. Thank the stars for the witches who came out and made light work of heavy lifting. Of course, I made sure that Dax and any other non-magical people who weren't in the loop on our secret of the coven were staying busy. There was no way to explain props floating into place or just plain appeared from thin air.

From across the hall, I noticed Gretchen Wilson, a local real estate agent whom I had suspected of being involved with Teddy Roberts' death, was pitching in too. I waved and she smiled back. It was good to see her out and about. Which reminded me to add a note on my phone about how Aunt Mimi made every spell appear effortless. But that tutorial would have to wait until after Halloween was over.

I blew the whistle which dangled from a cord around my neck. Gage had given it to me as a joke but since I couldn't project my voice above the din, this was the best way to get everyone's attention. Silence enveloped the grange hall and every volunteer turned to face me.

"Before we wrap up today, I'd like to go over the check-list so we know what has to be finished overnight. A few kind souls have volunteered to stay with Corbin until the last cobweb and bat are hung."

A loud round of applause broke out for Corbin, and of course people would guess Gage, Nikki, Steve, and Dax would be right beside me as I pledged from the beginning to be here all night if necessary so that we would open on time. I gave them a wide smile and Aunt Mimi said, "If anyone else wants to stay, pizza is on me."

Flashing her a grateful look, I knew she must want to get home and spend time with her new husband Nate, but he nodded as he stood next to her. They went together like a full moon and the stars on a frosty fall night.

"Alright, so I'll take a moment to review the list of scenes and who's going to be running them. If you need anything else for your area, now is the time to speak up." Everyone remained quiet so I kept going. "During kiddie hour, there will be no one popping out from behind curtains, nothing bubbling out of cauldrons." I gave Mimi a pointed look since she had just winked at Nate. "Vampires will remain with coffin lids closed and the mummy and various witches will not scare anyone." Giving a sharp look around the group, I said, "Clear?"

"Crystal like the ball, clear."

I recognized the deep gravelly voice, but I wasn't sure where Milo was hiding. On top of that, a crystal ball wasn't always clear. I chose to ignore the comment.

"Now, after eight is when the spooks come out. It will be dark and we'll have signs posted that people should enter at their own risk. In other words, if kids go in and get scared, that is not on this committee."

I could hear the murmur of agreement rumble through

the group. "Nikki has been working on carving one hundred pumpkins, but she could use help getting them into place and we're using battery-operated candles. Before you jump in to place them, see her for guidance." I ran my gaze down the length of the clipboard and didn't see anything else that I hadn't checked off. Without looking up, I asked, "Any questions?"

"Just one." A man I didn't recognize was standing next to Gretchen, and he stepped forward.

"Yes?"

"I'm Victor Seidel and I'm new to town. I was wondering if you could use an extra hand tomorrow night. Acting is my passion and Halloween, well, that's my time of year. I'm a great vampire."

"We already have a vampire." I glanced at Dax.

He took a step forward. "Lily, it's okay if Victor wants to be the coffin guy. I'm flexible. I can be a wizard who reads a crystal ball or something."

Aunt Mimi's eyes widened. "Fortune tellers are typically women."

He glanced her way. "True but we are in the twenty-first century and there are men who might be sensitive enough to read a crystal ball."

"Aunt Mimi, he has a point." I made a note on my clipboard. "Dax, you're our newest crystal ball expert."

"I will give great fortunes to anyone who wants to sit with me, just wait and see." He stepped back as if he wanted to blend in with the crowd.

"Victor, welcome to our little band of mischief and magic makers." I scanned the group. "But remember, people, scares and dares don't equal fun for little ones. Let's roll up our sleeves and wrap this up for tonight and call it a day."

. . .

The next morning the sky was a deep blue and the nip in the air stung my nose. I hurried to my car with Milo close on my heels. I opened the car door and he hopped into the passenger seat. Sliding behind the wheel, I buckled my seat belt before looking at him. "Why don't you stay home today or better yet hang out at the bookstore where you can take a catnap in the window?"

He gave me the one-eyed blink which was never a good sign coming from him. "If you insist on running this mockery of All Hallows Eve, I will be there in case you need something from me. After all, as your familiar, it is my sworn duty to help you in any way I can."

"What did you swear on, a stack of fish?" I laughed at my own joke.

"Puh-leeze. Being your familiar is most difficult. You're behind in your studies since you started your training late in life and you're determined to divide your time between work, your magic lessons, and Detective Cutie. I must take advantage of any free moments you have to continue your education."

"Fair enough." I started the car. "But I thought you wanted me and Gage to date."

"Of course I do. The man makes you smile. Above all, part of my role is to make sure you have a happy life."

I rubbed the top of his head. "Milo, you're really a softie."

He hissed. "Do not tell a soul. I'd get run out of the familiar union."

I did a double take. "There's a union?" What else did Milo know that I didn't?

Before I could ask more questions, he said, "Drive."

It wasn't long before I was parked in front of the grange hall. I was surprised to see the front door ajar. Had I forgotten to lock it last night when we left? I hoped none of the decorations had been disturbed by any breeze blowing in. The cobwebs were delicate, and I didn't have time to redo everything. But if needed, a spell or two could fix things up.

I hurried up the path and Milo ran off in the opposite direction toward the police station. As I walked inside and flicked on the overhead lights, a shiver raced down my spine as the spooky mood music kicked in. Even with daylight peeking through the gaps of the heavy curtains covering the windows, it was very spooky. "Hello. Is anyone here?" I walked deeper into the space. The silence was deafening. In another way that was comforting. I walked past each scene and took note it all looked exactly the same as when I left last night. I sighed in relief and then paused to look at Dax's table with the crystal ball placed dead center and a ladderback chair behind it. His back would be toward the curtain. I was hoping he'd keep an eye out to make sure there were no mischief makers. Tonight was about fun.

I sighed when I strolled by the vampire's coffin and hoped it wouldn't be too scary for the younger kids when they walked through. But Victor seemed to be on board with a gentle approach for the first hour. He was committed to handing out candy in his costume and skip the fangs until it was time for the adults.

. . .

Two hours later, volunteers began to arrive and all were dressed in their costumes. I slipped into the back and dressed in a long dark-purple velvet dress that I had embellished with moon and star appliques. The witches hat I wore was the same color and design. Despite not yet learning how to fly, I had a broom in one hand and a small black book with the word *spells* in gold paint across the front. It was blank and all for effect, but I thought this was a nice touch since my own powers were being discovered daily.

Aunt Mimi walked in dressed as a traditional witch and Nate was a wizard—so much for being her sidekick. She fluttered her fingers in the air and soft, spooky music filled the room and with another flick of her wrist all the mood lights came on and pumpkins were illuminated. I needed to work on that next. I could light real candles with a breath and intention, but to harness electricity, that was a different page in the book.

Nikki and Steve came in next and they were dressed up like mummies. Entwined in their bandages were colorful flowers but she had filled me in on her secret; she'd put a spell on the blooms and after eight they would become dried up and look like they had been dug up from a cemetery. I couldn't picture it but trusted she knew what she was doing. Behind them was Dax, wearing a wizard outfit that had me stop short. If he was local I would have guessed it wasn't a costume but that he was part of our magical community. He had a distinct air about him that was, dare I think, magical. I hurried over to give everyone a hug and thank them again for helping.

Nikki said, "We have a long line of excited families just outside the door."

"We're just waiting for Victor and Gage to arrive; everyone else is in place." The door opened and Gage strode in wearing a tan turtleneck and matching pants, and jutting from the top of his head was the end of a broomstick. When I laid eyes on him and laughed his eyes lit up the moment he saw me.

He brushed my cheek with his lips. "How's this for a couples costume?"

"I didn't know we were doing that. But you look great!" I took another look and said, "Is this your way of showing the world you're my steady sidekick?"

"My lady is a witch and you wanted to dress up so I figured why not come as your broom. But I can't take credit for the idea; it was all my mom."

I looked around. "Where are Glinda and Burke? I don't want to start without them."

"Dad was parking the car so they'll be right along." He took in my outfit. "You look great but no black?"

"I'm channeling my intuition tonight to make sure all is running smoothly and purple is a good conduit; at least that's what my book said when I consulted it."

He pecked my cheek. "No matter what color you wear, you're always the prettiest witch I know."

"Thank you." Warmth rushed to my cheeks and I took that moment to wave to Glinda and Burke who had come in and taken their spots in the ghost scene. "Everyone is here so let's open the doors and get this party started."

Gage and I welcomed each group of families as they entered and directed them to follow the glow-in-the-dark arrows that served as a guide through the event. Squeals of delight came from the kids as they bumped into clowns who wandered around. They weren't jumping out but I figured the kids were riding the wave of excitement. It was going great and when I looked at my watch, we were about thirty minutes into the event when a high-pitched scream pierced the night.

My hand gripped Gage's arm and I grinned. "Whoever just got scared must have a low threshold for fear."

He chuckled. "I hope we hear a lot more of that tonight."

A few more screams drifted our way, and I wondered what scene was causing the ruckus. It sounded as if it was coming from the vampire area and if the night kept up like this, our haunted house would be one people talked about for years to come. I turned to welcome the next group.

The pace of families entering had slowed and large groups of teens and adults were queuing up for our second act when we were going to do our best to scare people.

Victor came rushing toward me. "Lily, come quick! A clown collapsed right near me, and I don't know CPR."

I picked up the skirt of my dress and hurried after Victor with Gage beside me. He was on his cell phone calling for the emergency squad. My heart was in my throat. Our roaming clowns were two of Gage's police officers, Mac Sullivan and Sharon Peabody, and I prayed one of them wasn't sick. With any luck, it was just overheating from the costume and mask. As we rounded the final bend in the path, there were two clowns on the floor, kneeling next to another person in a clown costume as they performed CPR. I breathed a sigh of relief when I recognized Mac and Sharon. The mask was off the other person and I knew who he was—Malcom Sloane, a regular customer in The Cozy Nook Bookshop.

"We've called for the ambulance," I shouted over the mood music.

Peabody counted off, "Twenty-nine, thirty." She

stopped compressions, then Mac gave two breaths and she began again.

While she counted, Mac glanced at Gage. "No pulse when we got his mask off."

"Heart attack?" he asked.

"Possibly." Mac was ready to administer the two breaths again.

Victor's breathing was coming in short, ragged gasps. "I went behind the curtain to get more candy for the kids. I was only gone a second and someone screamed. I assumed it was the coffin lid opening, but when I came back, the clown was on the ground, toes up."

No pulse equaled dead to me. Gage looked around the group of horrified families. "Lily. Would you take everyone here to the back room and give them some refreshments? And see if you can get my parents to close the doors until we get a handle on this situation."

I mentally called to Aunt Mimi to meet me in the back, thanking the stars this was one spell I could work with success every time. I ushered the children and their parents down the short corridor and into the old-fashioned kitchen where we had cups of cider and donuts already laid out.

Aunt Mimi and Nate bustled in and took one look at the group and said, "We've got this; you're needed in the front."

I walked quickly to where Glinda and Burke were stationed and whispered, "Can you cover the door? Don't let anyone in except the EMTs. It appears a clown had a heart attack."

"Whatever you need," Burke said.

Even as I said those words, doubt began to creep in. What was Malcom doing dressed in costume at the event?

When he had been in the store a few days ago, I asked if he could volunteer, and he said he didn't have time to help but he'd pencil me in for the next holiday event. So, if he couldn't volunteer tonight, why was he lying on the floor, probably dead?

Chapter 3

Gage

This wasn't what Lily or anyone in our small town needed tonight. A real dead person at a haunted house. The irony was too much. I heard people running in our direction and assumed it would be the emergency team. They could take over and I'd have Mac and Peabody talk to the families who had witnessed the event. It shouldn't take long to get statements and let families go on their way.

I stepped aside to make room for emergency personnel. My eyes met Lily's, who was across the aisle from me. She was standing next to Victor whose mouth was moving but I couldn't hear what he was saying. Not that it mattered. A clown had a heart attack and died in front of some poor kids. What a Halloween for them to remember.

As the EMTs used the defibrillator to kick-start Malcom's heart, the tension grew. I saw the grim look on Peabody and Mac's faces. They had been around long enough to know that things weren't looking great for a positive outcome. After trying for what seemed like an eternity, Suzi, the EMT handling the resuscitator bag, looked at me and gave a short shake of her head. "Can you bring in the stretcher? We need to transport him."

Mac was already moving toward the exit to get it.

"Thoughts? Heart?" Before she could answer, I noticed the small pool of thick, red liquid seeping from under the voluminous clown costume. "Peabody, any mention anyone heard anything?"

Stew, who had been using the defibrillator handles, rolled Malcom to the side and said, "Looks as if it was a gunshot based on the cloth."

Not that I wanted to lead with conjecture, but considering the amount of blood our victim had lost, he was probably already dead before he landed. "You didn't notice any blood when you were doing CPR?"

Peabody said, "No."

Stew was checking for a pulse again. "If the bullet acted as a plug in the entrance wound, once he was shocked it would come loose and the blood would start to migrate outward. But the medical examiner will know more after the autopsy."

Lily was staring at me. The last thing I wanted to do was end the event, but it had to be done. "We'll need to shut down the haunted house. It's now an active crime scene." I gave a hard look to Victor. "I'd appreciate if you'd stay put for now. I'm hoping you saw something that will help us figure out who killed Mr. Sloane."

His head bobbed up and down like one of those bobblehead dolls you see in a car or truck where the head bounces around on a spring. "Peabody, check to see how many families are left in the kitchen and once it's cleared, escort Victor and the rest of the volunteers in there. We need to do a preliminary round of questioning while everything is still fresh in our minds."

Mac was back with the gurney, sliding it over the wide plank wood floor. When he came to a stop, he unbuckled the straps. Within moments, Suzi and Stew had loaded the victim and covered him with a sheet. I glanced at Lily and wished I could have shielded her from this but more importantly I'd like to know why our body count in town was growing faster than lobsters coming off Nate's fishing boat.

Victor's voice cracked. "I think I need to go home. This has all been too much for me to handle."

With laser-like focus on his face, I said, "I need to ask a few questions first." I wondered where Dax was in all the commotion. I could use his help in securing the scene since my officers were headed to talk with the families in the kitchen.

Lily tipped her head. "Dax?"

I nodded and found it comforting that we were on the same wavelength. She moved in the direction to where he should be. The gurney was raised and before Stew could push it out the front door, I stopped Suzi. "Can we use the emergency exit to shield the bystanders and give Malcom some dignity as he's wheeled out?"

She nodded and I pulled back one of the black curtains to a partially obscured exit door. Lily had liked that we had so many exits; in case anyone got scared, they could slip out. Never did I imagine one would be used for this. Once the EMTs were outside and had loaded the gurney in the back of the ambulance, I secured it again and returned to Victor. "Can you tell me what happened?"

He wrung his hands. As far I was concerned, he was far too nervous to be a vampire in a haunted house. And he was new to town. Had his sole purpose here been to shoot Malcom? That might have been far-fetched, but I needed to keep him on my active suspect list. And as of this moment, my only real suspect.

His gaze darted around the scene, almost as if he was trying to confirm we were alone. "It's like I said, I was running out of candy and wanted to refill the bowl. I had noticed the clown a few times hovering around my area and to be honest, I thought he was one of us. A volunteer."

I nodded, wanting him to continue but I didn't want to add more pressure to the situation so he'd clam up.

"There had been so many kids taking handfuls of candy and they just kept coming..." He licked his lips. "I was gone for less than a minute and I heard something, like a heavy book hitting the floor. A kid screamed and that's when I saw the clown on the ground."

"The term you used was toes up." It indicated a backward fall which made sense since he had been shot from behind and the shooter pulled him back so no one would notice the blood, giving him or her time to escape.

"Yeah, he was flat on his back. Then another person screamed, and then the other two clowns appeared and started CPR. It was like a movie in fast-forward but still seemed to take forever, if you know what I mean?"

I understood where he was coming from but continued to play the cool, noncommittal cop.

Dax strode up with Lily. "Gage, I understand we have a situation?"

"Yes. Would you go with Lily and announce the event has been closed for the evening? As soon as we've cleared the scene, we'll reopen it, most likely in a few days." I gave Lily a quick look and she nodded. "And switch the overhead lights on, please and kill the sound effects."

"You got it. We'll be back as soon as we can." Dax ushered Lily ahead of him down the hall and I turned back to Victor. "Was there anyone else besides the clown loitering?"

The overhead lights flicked on and the chilling moans stopped, causing Victor to blink several times while his eyes adjusted to the brightness. It was then I noticed the lid on the fake coffin was ajar. Not going any closer, I surveyed the scene, wishing I had a flashlight to get a better look.

"I thought you weren't going to start coming out of the coffin until after the little ones were done?" Maybe that was why we had heard more screams than we expected.

"I haven't been in the coffin since last night when we made sure the hinge worked smoothly. And when I got here tonight, I opened and closed it just to double-check. I wouldn't have deliberately scared the kids. That would just be downright mean."

We agreed on one thing. Withdrawing my cell phone, I texted Peabody, telling her I needed her back at the crime scene. Next, I texted the station to get a cruiser en route since no one had arrived yet. I couldn't imagine what the holdup was. She responded she was on her way and that Jonesy and Shepard were on duty tonight. That still didn't explain where they were.

Dax and Lily came back. He said, "What's going on?"

Lily walked the wood border which delineated where vampire haven started. "Gage, come, take a look."

"I saw the lid."

She looked over her shoulder. Her face was drawn and her lips were in a thin line. "That's not it. I think there's a handgun partially hidden under the ferns. Whoever shot Malcom must have dropped it while they were escaping."

"This might be the break we need. Don't touch it. With any luck the perp will have left fingerprints." She glared at me, and I realized what I had said. "Sorry, Lily, force of habit. I know you'd never contaminate a crime scene."

The sound of police sirens grew closer and finally we could begin to gather the evidence. My phone vibrated and the message was from Mac asking me to come to the kitchen. There was a father who had an interesting story that I had to hear.

"Lily, want to come with me? Dax can wait for the officers. Let them know Peabody will assist them."

"You got it."

Lily fell into step beside me. "What's going on?"

"Mac texted and said there could be some new information." As we entered the kitchen, there were only a few family groups left. Mac was with Kevin Valentine and his daughter, Josie. Kevin had taken over his family's business, Bygone Antiques, when his parents retired a few years back and he was active in the community. Josie was sitting on a stool, dressed as an adorable little witch with long blond curls spilling down her back from under her black pointy hat. She was sipping cider and munching on a donut. Hopefully the distraction eased what she had witnessed earlier. Kevin saw me looking at him, but he didn't look away. His cool and steady gaze had an air of challenge in it.

He crossed the room and I shook his hand. "Kevin. I hope your daughter is okay?"

"Thanks, I don't know if she realized what happened. As soon as I saw the clown falling, I put her behind me. Even with the screaming, she thought it was all part of the fun." He glanced her way. "Can we move toward the door? I don't want Josie to hear us talking."

"Of course."

"Josie, I'm going to talk to Detective Gage for a minute. Finish your treats, and then we can go home, okay?"

Her sunny smile was a welcome change from the heavy atmosphere. "Sure, Daddy."

Lily walked with us and if Kevin thought it was odd, he never mentioned it. Positioning himself so he could keep an eye on Josie while we talked, he said, "We were strolling through the haunted house. Josie likes to take her time and look at everything. Nothing scares her. The scenes are more like a puzzle to her; she wants to know how everything works. Not that how Josie looks at things is the point. While we were taking our time, other families were going around us; kids were getting spooked, but I noticed a few clowns walking around."

"How many is a few?" Lily asked.

"Four, I think, maybe five, I'm not sure now. I know that two were Sharon and Mac but the other two near the vampire's coffin were a mystery. They seemed to step into the shadows together and back out again and one said boo. It was kind of creepy but of course Josie thought it was a hoot. What's not to love about clowns, right?"

I looked at Lily but she didn't speak or even glance my way. We only had two clowns that should have been at the event as helpers. So other than our dead clown, who was the other one or two?

"Anyway, we were standing in front of the vampire display when the actor picked up the half-full bowl of candy and said he needed to refill it. There was still plenty, but that's when Josie tugged on my hand and pointed to the lid on the coffin. It was moving."

Lily leaned forward. "Are you sure?"

"Josie actually giggled and asked me if someone was going to pop out and try to scare us."

"That didn't bother her at all?" I asked, surprised that a six-year-old kid would be so blasé about the whole thing.

"Nothing fazes her. It's like the fear part of her brain never kicked on. Like I said, it's all about figuring out who is doing what and how."

Mac had been right; this was important information. "Where was our resident vampire during this?"

"He hadn't come back yet, and Josie wanted to see what candy he was getting so she asked if we could wait. Honestly, I was ready to move on."

"Did the lid go back down?" Lily wasn't going to let him get derailed.

"No. It was placed back sort of half-open, half-closed. But no one ever appeared. I figured it was just a moving prop like some of the other scenes had. It was then a clown brushed past me, jostling Josie without saying excuse me. I try to teach her good manners, but it's hard when adults don't use them."

Again, he was veering off the topic and I'm sure it was due to the stress of what had happened. Being so close to someone dying did that to a person, but in his defense, he didn't know anyone had died.

"That was when the clown fell to the floor, the vampire came back, and I noticed the lid on the coffin had gone back into place. Then the screaming."

"Did you notice anything else?" Lily's brows furrowed together as I knew she was walking the steps through her head.

"No. Once we came in here to wait I told Mac what happened, he said you'd want to talk to me." He looked at his little girl who had finished licking glaze off her fingertips. "Is it okay if we take off? There is a little witch who looks like she could use a bath."

I clapped Kevin on the shoulder. "Thanks for the information and if I have more questions, is it okay to swing by the store?"

"Anytime. I'm either there or at home. The glamorous life of a single dad."

Lily said, "I'm glad Josie is alright. Seeing someone die right in front of her could have been quite a shock."

Kevin's eyes grew wide. "Malcom died?"

She looked at me and said, "He did."

"Wow, a heart attack on Halloween. I wonder if he'll become a ghost. You know since he was hovering all night; he must have unfinished business."

Josie might not be fazed by things that pretended to go bump in the night, but her father was.

"If you remember anything else, give me a call." I pulled out a business card from my wallet and handed it to him. "It has my contact information at the station."

"Will do. And it's too bad this all happened, Lily. Your haunted house is the best we've had around here in a long time."

"Thank you. We hope to reopen it once all this is cleared up. Come back and finish the tour."

Kevin gave her a guarded smile. "Probably not. One haunted house a year is my limit."

Chapter 4
Lily

Gage and I watched as Kevin plucked Josie off the stool. He carried her out the back entrance since the door leading to the interior hall was blocked by a police officer. A few thoughts were spinning in my head, but I wanted to jot them down on my clue board before I said anything to Gage. I glanced in his direction. "Do you think we'll learn anything more tonight?"

Gage dropped his arm around my shoulders and gave me a comforting one-armed hug. "Probably not. We'll have to wait on the autopsy to learn more about the gunshot and why the blood took so long to seep out. Could he have been saved if they hadn't used the defibrillator on him?"

"Don't go second-guessing yourself. Mac said there was no pulse. He may have died instantly." I wasn't sure if that was rare but had the bullet created a tamponade if it had hit the heart? Speculation was my strength, but from the weary look on Gage's face, tonight wasn't the time nor the place to start spinning questions.

He reached up to rub a hand over his head and pulled the broom head sticking out from his jacket. "You're right.

It's best to wait for the report. We should send our families home and you should go too. It's going to be a long night."

I took the broom and waved it from side to side. "Do you want me to sweep everyone along?"

He gave me a small, exhausted smile. "That's not necessary, but I'll walk you to your car. Do me a favor, and shoot me a text when you get home safe."

After sending everyone home with a promise that Gage and I would touch base tomorrow, Nikki and Steve followed me home. They pulled in behind me after I parked in front of the garage. With a flick of Nikki's wrist, she turned the lights on in the house. I for sure was going to learn that spell next. It would be nice to always enter a brightly lit house.

"Coffee? Tea? Cocoa?" I held the door open while they came inside.

Nikki said, "Cocoa sounds delicious, but I'll make it. It's been a rough night." She unwrapped some of her mummy bandages and pointed to a chair. "Sit."

I noticed Steve was taking his costume off. "Thanks again for helping out." I dropped into a chair, weary from the insanity of the last few days all to be overshadowed by a murder.

Milo trotted into the room and hopped up into my lap. He headbutted my chin with his soft gray head. "Lily, are you okay? I heard there was trouble at the hall."

I scratched under his chin and around his ears. There were times when he knew exactly what I needed and it soothed my soul. "How did you hear so quickly?"

"Familiar network." He purred and turned his head so I could easily scratch the other side of his face.

Softly, I chuckled. "Of course, there's a network for your kind. Did anyone mention seeing anything that might be helpful?"

He bent his neck forward, and I scratched behind his ears. "No. Since this was a human event, we snuck in, but we didn't stay long—too mundane for us."

Nikki grinned. "You'll get used to the familiars thinking we're boring." She placed three mugs of decadent steaming cocoa on the table, complete with whipped cream.

"I didn't..." But I didn't finish that thought. As a kitchen witch Nikki could whip up anything from thin air. "I wish I was better in the kitchen."

Milo looked at me through slitted eyes. "Me too. Your fish is usually dry."

"Hey." I placed him on the floor. "For that, go scratch your own ears."

He swished his tail and pranced from the room, but not before muttering, "A little constructive criticism gets you nowhere."

I was too tired for a snappy retort. Besides, all I wanted to do was pull out my clue board and write down what I remembered while it was still fresh. But first cocoa. I took a tentative sip, unsure how hot it might be, but as usual it was perfect. "Nikki, this is amazing."

Steve grinned. "That's my future wife." He took a big drink and when he set his mug down, a dollop of cream was on his nose.

I couldn't help but laugh and flipped a paper napkin at him. "You're a goof. Keep that up and she might not marry you."

Nikki took his hand and batted her eyelashes at him. "Fat chance. He's my person."

The lovebirds gazed into each other's eyes and I got up

to pull out the chalkboard. "Before you get carried away with lovey stuff, let's talk about what happened tonight and what you might have seen."

Steve jumped up. "Let me help you."

I dug through the junk drawer in search of chalk. With a snap of her fingers, Nikki handed me a piece and then grinned.

"Now, why didn't I think of that?"

"You're still in the habit of thinking like a non-magical person. That will change with time and as you learn spells which help around the house."

I was glad one of us was confident in my long-term ability. I wiped the board clean by moving my hand in a lateral motion from one side of the blackboard to the other. It took more concentration than what Nikki exhibited, but it was a good start.

"See, you're doing great."

I smiled and took another sip of the cocoa. "I'll share what I know, and you can fill in any blanks. Right now, we have nothing to go on so any tiny detail might help."

They both nodded and waited while I wrote Malcom's name across the top.

Pausing, I tapped the chalk on my chin before I began to jot down notes. "We heard the screams and Gage and I rushed to the vampire section. There was a clown on the ground, with Peabody and Mac performing CPR. Mac said he hadn't felt a pulse, but they kept trying." Steve and Nikki's fingers were entwined, but their attention was focused on the board. "Between you and me, if anyone could have restarted that man's heart, it would have been that dynamic duo. It was only after the EMTs shocked him that he started to bleed from what turned out to be a gunshot wound to his back." I didn't pause for effect, but kept writing down bullet points. "Here's where it gets interesting. A couple of days ago, I asked Malcom if he wanted to help out. He said he couldn't that he was busy. So why was he there and in costume? And there was another clown wandering around, but nobody knows who it was or where they went."

I added *Clown #2 Unknown* to the board.

"Now remember how we all agreed that the scary stuff would be left for after the family groups had come and gone?"

Nikki and Steve nodded. She tipped her head and narrowed her eyes. "What happened?"

"Josie Valentine said the coffin lid was moving before the clown fell."

Steve sat up straighter in his chair. "What was Victor thinking, trying to scare those munchkins? We shouldn't let him help again if he can't follow the rules."

I held up my hand to stop him for now. "There's one of two possibilities. Either Victor was looking to add some thrills to his scene for some reason or the killer was in the coffin."

With a snap of her fingers, Nikki said, "Or Victor is the killer."

I nodded and added question mark next to Victor's name. "First, we need to figure out why was Malcom there, who had a motive for killing him, and who the other clown was and where he went." Adding a few more cryptic notes to the board, I added *gun*.

"And there was a gun next to the coffin, partially hidden under some ferns that Victor specifically asked to have placed around the scene."

"What do we know about him?" Steve asked.

I held back a smile. Steve had caught the sleuth bug

after he had gone out to Dean Hartley's place when Nikki and I were following up on a few clues. "Not much. He's only lived in town for about a year. He keeps to himself, and this is the first time he's volunteered. Now Malcom is also quiet, but he's lived here a lot longer. He always seemed very nice when he came into the bookshop."

"I wonder," Nikki drawled, "when did Dax say the fraud case really kicked off in this part of Maine?"

That was an interesting thread. "It has to have been a while, since it was going on before Flora was killed. It was one of the secrets she was using to put the squeeze on residents and Teddy Roberts, and remember, our second murder in town was a part of the fraud case."

I wrote down *real estate*. "It's probably a stretch but this could be tied into that mess. Dax said the case is cold and he's been waiting for something to pop."

Nikki asked, "Does anyone know what Malcom did for a living?"

"Freelance writer, I think," Steve said. "When he brought his car in to be fixed a month ago, he was working on an article that he said was due that day so he brought his laptop and worked in the lobby."

I added *freelance writer* next to his name. "But we still don't know what Victor does or why he even relocated to Pembroke Cove."

I set the chalk down and wiped my fingertips on a paper napkin. "Based on the clues, these are major questions for us to investigate. Tomorrow I'm going to drop by Victor's, just to see how he's feeling after the shock tonight, and I'll try to discover what he does for work. Once I know that, maybe Gage will have answers about the gun and if we're real lucky, the identity of the other clown."

Steve drained the last of his cocoa and stifled a yawn. "Ready to go home, Nik?"

She stood and gave me a hug. "Are you going to be okay? We can stay over if you want."

I hugged her tight. "I'm fine. Besides, this case has nothing to do with me and if I need help, I have Milo. Sort of."

With a laugh, she said, "He'll remind you to read your book, *Practical Beginnings*."

"I'm going to do some reading. I want to see if it will finally show me how to do something useful, like turn lights on and off."

I walked them to the door and promised to call if I needed anything. Once they backed out of the driveway, I checked the locks on the front and back doors before retrieving my spell book. I got ready for bed and crawled in. Milo hopped up and gave me a nod of approval when he saw I had my book in my lap.

With his sweet low kitty growl, he said, "That's a sight for these green eyes."

I found it humorous he had to mention what color his eyes were, as if I had missed it over the last few years. But sometimes he just liked it when I noticed something about him. "You have the greenest eyes of any cat I've seen."

He puffed out his chest. "It's because I'm one in a zillion."

I pulled him close and kissed the top of his head. "Yes, you are. Now if you'd take a snooze, I can get some reading done." I set him on the pillow next to me and he walked around in circles until he settled in. Within seconds, soft kitty snores reached my ears.

I flicked open the book and leafed through the first few pages. The summoning spell, banishing spell, levitation, and lighting a candle all brought a smile to my face. My favorite was the protection spell, but they had all come in handy over the last several months. What would I learn next? I closed my eyes and whispered, "Please let me master some basics—lights, opening a jar, or fixing something that is broken. I ask this with pure heart, so shall it be." I kept my eyes closed for a few more minutes for good measure.

I opened them and when I did, the pages of the book turned slowly, as if the book was thinking what should come next. The pages stopped moving and in front of me was the spell for turning lights on and off. Finally. I couldn't help but grin.

I read the spell over several times. "This seems easy. Just concentrate on flipping the light switch up or down and ask for it to be. Does that mean I make up my own spell for it to work since there isn't a specific incantation?"

What would be easy for me to remember, especially if I ever came under a stressful situation and needed to turn the lights on or off? The words would need to roll off my tongue but still kind of rhyme. "Lights on or lights off. The opposite of what is, is what shall be."

That didn't sound half-bad. Now to see if it would work. I looked across the room at the light switch. The two lamps were on that one switch so if this worked my bedroom would be plunged in darkness and maybe I could call it a day. I thought of how easy Aunt Mimi and Nikki had made it look, and here I was fretting over it working.

I concentrated on being surrounded by the night. In a clear, loud voice, I said, "Lights on or lights off. The opposite of what is, is what shall be." My room was still illuminated. Dang. I flicked back the covers and got out of my cozy bed. This time I held my palms up and repeated myself, solely focused on darkness blanketing me. The lights in my bedroom went dark, but I expected to see the streetlight shining in my window. I rushed to the glass and looked up and down the street. Not only had I extinguished lights at my house, but it appeared I turned them off on my street. Who knew that was possible? I took a step back from the glass, and with palms up, I changed up the words. "Lights off, turn on. The opposite of is, is what shall be."

Still dark.

"My dear witch, what are you doing?"

My heart began to race. How was I going to fix this? "Milo, hush. I have to think. I was working on a spell to turn the bedroom lights on and off and it seems I've shut down the streetlights too."

If a cat could laugh hysterically, it would be mine. I could see a faint outline of him rolling on his back, legs up in the air, making the most awful caterwaul kind of noise.

"Do you mind? I have to fix this before a non-magical person notices this isn't a natural blackout."

My phone rang and Milo said, "Too late. Detective Cutie is calling to check on you. Are you going to fess up this was your handiwork?"

Ignoring him, I picked up my phone. "Gage, is everything alright?"

"Yes, but I wanted to make sure that you were okay. Seems the power is out all over town."

I smacked my hand to my forehead. "Any idea how that happened?"

"No, but I'm sure the electric company will get it sorted out soon. If you need anything, just call. I'm headed home."

"Thanks. Be careful driving and we'll talk tomorrow."

"Good night, sweetheart."

Once we disconnected, I quickly dialed Aunt Mimi. The moment the lines were connected, she said, "Let me guess. A new spell has plunged the town into darkness?" Behind her words was laughter.

"Yes, Aunt Mimi. Any chance you can pop over and help me sort this out?"

"I'll be there shortly. But Lily, I don't want you to lose heart. Once you master this spell, others will fall into place."

"I'm glad one of us is confident. Controlling lights could be fun."

Milo was still laughing. "One could say even illuminating."

Chapter 5
Lily

The next morning with the electricity restored, thanks to Aunt Mimi's tutelage, Milo and I walked toward my bookstore in the crisp air. The sun was out but it wasn't providing much warmth. When I was unlocking the door, I noticed Victor sitting on a bench in Park Square. I lifted my hand and waved but he didn't seem to notice or was he ignoring me? Only one way to find out and it would save me a trip out to his place.

I ushered Milo inside, turned on all the lights, and dropped my bags in the wingback chair near the door. "Be back in a jiff."

He called after me, "Take your time. I've got nothing going on today".

I locked the door and stashed the old metal key in my jacket pocket. I ran my hand over my short hair, making sure to appear unruffled, and walked across the grass, my boots crunching over the frosty surface.

"Victor, good morning." I made sure a friendly smile graced my face. "How are you?"

He lifted his head, his eyes wary. "What are you doing here?"

I gestured to my store. "I was going to work and noticed you sitting here. I waved but I guess you didn't see me."

"Maybe I want to be left alone."

Settling on the cold bench next to him, I ignored that last statement. "I was going to check in with you today, after last night. We all had quite a shock."

"Why?" The word seemed to be a snarl; there was nothing pleasant in his tone of voice or demeanor.

Taken aback, I gave him a long look. "Someone died, a member of our community, and you were there when it happened. I'm sure it was as shocking for you as it was to me when we discovered he had been shot."

He interlaced his fingers and stared at his clasped hands. "I didn't know the guy well, we met a couple of times."

"He was a kind man, quiet and unassuming."

With a sharp look, he said, "A clown costume really doesn't suit that personality."

I hadn't thought the type of costume would be relevant. "Maybe under the quiet façade, he was a jokester and it didn't come out often."

Victor laced and unlaced his fingers again. "There's no way to know now."

"Did you know he was a freelance writer?"

Victor's hands formed into fists, his knuckles growing white. "I had no idea, I didn't know him remember and who knows what anyone does in this town."

Here was an opening and I seized it. "I own a bookstore. What do you do?"

"Real estate development."

My mouth went dry. "In Pembroke Cove?"

"Nah, too small of an area. Primarily hotels, casinos, you know big moneymakers. I moved here to live a quiet life when I'm between projects."

My heartbeat thumped in my chest. Had I just stumbled across Dax's missing connection? Eager to appear nonchalant, I asked, "How do you like it here?"

"It's quaint. I'd like to get more involved with town politics. I have ideas to improve the tourist business which in turn would generate higher revenues for small businesses like yours."

"That's something we've always struggled with here, but we like our close-knit community. In the summer, like most areas in Maine, we get more tourists."

"Wouldn't it be nice to draw them in year-round?"

"I guess." I shifted on the cold, hard bench. "What are you working on now?"

"I'm waiting for some pieces to fall into place on a parcel of land I'm trying to acquire, but there have been a few stumbling blocks." He gave me a side-glance. "But I'm a patient man."

A shiver raced down my back. Was he patient enough to wait until the smoke had cleared from Malcom's murder before kick-starting his takeover of Pembroke Cove, and did he plan on turning it into another Atlantic City? Wait until I shared this insight with Gage and Dax. We needed to take a closer look at Victor.

Standing up, I noticed the stores around the square had opened up, flags were out, lights on, and people were ready to start their day. "I need to get back to work, but if you're looking for a good book, stop in sometime. I do special orders too."

"I'm not much of a reader, but I appreciate the offer." He stood and stuck out his hand. "Thank you."

"You're welcome." I wasn't sure what exactly he was thanking me for.

"People haven't been very welcoming since I arrived. It seems if you're not three generations deep, you're not accepted."

Softening a little from my previous thought that he was behind the real estate fraud, I said, "There are a few people like that, but the majority are friendly. You made a good start wanting to help out at the haunted house. Maybe pop into different stores and chat people up. To have friends, you have to be one."

He gave me a side glance. "Did your mother tell you that?"

I couldn't help but grin at the small smile tugging the corners of his mouth. "Yes, as a matter of fact, she did."

"Where's the best coffee in town?"

Playfully I shook my finger at him. "Nope, not going there since I like all the business owners, but if you're looking to pair coffee with something decadent, you should head over to The Sweet Spot. William makes the best pecan cinnamon rolls; you'll want to get two and save one for tomorrow. Just heat it up in the microwave for fifteen seconds and it's like fresh baked all over again."

He tapped two fingers to his forehead in a salute. "Thanks for the tip, Lily. I'll be seeing ya." He turned on his heel and headed in the direction of the bakery.

I withdrew my cell and typed a message to Gage and Dax. *Bookstore ASAP. I have new information that could be useful.* The device made a whoosh sound and I slipped it back into my jacket pocket and hurried back to my store.

. . .

Thirty minutes later, Gage and Dax walked into the bookstore.

Gage was carrying a bag that bore The Sweet Spot logo and a tray of what I assumed was coffee. He held the bag aloft. "I thought we could use a shot of sugar and caffeine to get us going after last night."

I took the coffee tray and set it on the small wood table in front of the wingback chairs. Dax was dragging another chair close. It was funny; we had our typical seats and didn't deviate from them.

Dax said, "Sorry it took a while. I was at the station talking with Gage about my case and there are a few things I'm trying to wrap up before I go."

"Go?" I looked from Dax to Gage.

Dax nodded. "Since the case seems to be cold, I'm going to head down to Louisiana to see my family for a bit, but I'll be back."

Cocking my head, I grinned. "You might want to hold off booking your flight. I have information that could change the direction of your case."

He handed me a to-go cup and a napkin. "I'm all ears."

Gage said, "Are you investigating already?"

I shrugged and then smiled. "When an opportunity presents itself, I seize it and Victor was sitting across from my store this morning when I was opening up and we had an amiable chat."

He shook his head. "You do know he's a suspect?"

"If he wasn't, he would be now. Do you know he's a real estate developer?"

Dax sat up straight. "What are you talking about? I thought he was a writer?"

I shook my head. "That would be Malcom, our victim.

He was a freelance writer, but Victor works in real estate development. He told me mostly hotels and casinos. Big money." I tipped my head to the side. "Could it be possible he's behind your case, trying to buy up property cheap to get the town to agree to some large hotels, maybe even a casino? That would change life here in Pembroke Cove."

"Possible." Dax's Southern drawl slipped out. "But we need to check with the town to see if something of that magnitude would even be considered."

Gage said, "Maybe he figures if he buys up all the property, he can pressure the town into granting him a special variance."

I sagged against the back of my chair. "To think our little town could become a gambling destination. I shudder to think what that would do to all the business owners, fishermen, and our way of life." What also crossed my mind, but I didn't mention it in the presence of my current company, was our magical community. It would displace so many witches that I hadn't even met yet, and what of the other magical beings that Nikki and Milo had alluded to last night? "We have to find out more about Victor."

Dax withdrew a pumpkin muffin from the bakery bag before handing it to me. "I can run him through my work database to see what is known. Once we get a handle on some basics, we'll know where to go from there."

"Gage, any idea about Malcom's death?"

He sipped his coffee as if gathering his thoughts. "Well, interestingly, the coffin had a false bottom and it looks like someone could lie in there undetected. We're sure based on the entrance wound Malcom was shot from someone in or near the coffin. Remember how Josie said the lid moved? My working theory is, someone was in the coffin waiting for him, shot him, and amid the chaos was able to slip out under the platform the coffin was on and blend in with the crowd."

I nibbled my muffin. That made sense, but why Malcom?

Dax asked, "But why Malcom and how did the shooter know they shot the right clown? We know there were four at the event last night."

"Possibly five, but at this point I think that was bad information." Gage rested his right ankle on his left knee. "Since two of those clowns are police officers, I hope they weren't the target. I thought of that angle and checked, and they haven't received any threats. Besides, it was common knowledge for anyone working the event where Peabody and Mac would be. But with other clowns roaming around, it is possible Malcom wasn't the target. However, until we know for sure, I'm going to proceed under the assumption he was. It's the most logical conclusion."

Dax and I nodded in agreement and I asked, "Where do we go from here?"

Gage gave me a look that I knew all too well and I also knew what he was about to say. "We don't go anywhere. There is a murderer in town. Please leave the investigation to the professionals. Dax will check into Victor's background, and I'll wait for the report from the medical examiner. You will sell some books, or better yet, read a good book." His brow quirked above his right eye and I knew what book he was referring to.

"I did some reading last night and all is up to date and proceeding nicely."

Popping the last of his muffin into his mouth, Dax said, "Hey, do you guys know what happened to the electricity last night? My power was out at the motel for about an hour."

"Mine too." I didn't dare look at Gage. He might puzzle together that somehow I was involved. At that moment Milo came slinking around the corner and rubbed up against Gage's leg.

"Yeah, I think it might have been a transformer," Gage said, scooping Milo up since he was meowing loudly.

"I figured it was only a matter of time before the blackout came up." Milo leaned into Gage's hand. "See, Lily, your detective has gotten the hang of paying attention to me too."

Dax's eyes widened briefly and then returned to normal.

"Milo can be chatty in the morning." Thank heavens Dax would only hear him meowing and I didn't dare look at Gage since he would know my familiar was talking to me. "Must have been an easy fix." I thought of Aunt Mimi helping me create the counter spell and it had been easy once I stopped panicking.

Gage got up from the chair and set Milo down before picking up the empty bag and cup tray. "I need to head back to the station. Dax, are you coming?"

"No. I'm going back to the motel to do some research. But I'll touch base later."

Not that either man had asked me what my plan was, I announced, "I'll get ready for my onslaught of customers and if anything happens on my end, I'll be sure to let you know."

"Lily," Gage dropped a kiss on my cheek, "The information you got from Victor was valuable, but I don't want you going around asking questions. Someone might want to stop you from getting too close to the truth, especially now that everyone in town knows you were instrumental in solving the last three major crimes."

In a small way, what Gage said was a compliment, but one of these days he was going to have to accept asking questions and puzzling out the truth was woven into my DNA, just like being a witch. "You have nothing to worry about. I won't be out questioning suspects." I crossed my fingers behind my back since I wasn't sure what my day would entail. One thing was for sure, I was going to find out what kind of a writer Malcom was and who he worked for. That would be very valuable.

After tossing the garbage in the back room, Gage strode to the front door. "I'll call you later."

"You know how to find me." I deliberately didn't say where, since if I got the notion to take off, Aunt Mimi or Nikki would cover the bookstore for me.

"Dax, I'll be in touch." He closed the door behind him.

Dax stretched his legs out in front of him as if he was planning on a longer visit. I stepped over them on my way to the desk and turned on my computer. I gave him a side-glance. "Is there something I can help you with?"

He got up and strolled to the counter. "What book were you reading last night? Maybe I should pick up a copy."

"A book on family history. Nothing you'd find interesting. But I could help you pick out something to read. How about *Ethan Frome*?"

"Read it, thought it was good, but I am fascinated by history." His eyes never left mine.

"History. Well, I have a robust section on the history of Pembroke Cove or Maine in general if you'd like."

"Not today. But tell me, are you going to check into Malcom's background as a writer?"

Chapter 6
Gage

I closed the door, leaving Dax with Lily in the bookstore. By the mischievous look in her eyes, she was already plotting and maybe he'd stick around long enough to make sure she stayed out of trouble. It was too early in the investigation for me to get distracted and besides, she had unearthed some very interesting information on Victor. Information I didn't even know yet, but I would have discovered. Who was I kidding? She had a gift for getting people to open up to her.

My gaze scanned the town park and I headed toward the police station and then went back to the grange hall. I couldn't figure out when someone had time to modify the coffin since Steve and I built that scene it was in. It just didn't make sense. When we discovered a section of plywood that was about a foot and a half wide that flipped down into the base, we knew someone could slip in and out but they needed to be thin. The entire bottom section of the coffin had been rebuilt, as if overnight. But the person needed to be comfortable with a tight fit or was a witch. I changed direction and walked to Tucker's Hardware. If anyone purchased a sheet of plywood in the last forty-eight hours, it might have come from the hardware store since he always carried a small supply.

The old-fashioned bell, attached to the door, jingled, announcing my arrival. Tucker, Mike Shaw, and Nate O'Brien were clustered around the front counter. They looked up as I entered, and conversation stilled. "Morning, gentlemen."

Nate said, "Morning, Detective."

When it was off hours and we saw each other socially, he called me Gage; otherwise, he seemed to want to make a point to others my role in our fair town.

"Can I help you with something?" Tucker moved from behind the counter.

"I was hoping you could tell me if you've sold a sheet of plywood in the last two days, and if yes, who purchased it."

He clasped his hands together and his brow furrowed. "As a matter of fact, I did. To Malcom Sloane."

That wasn't what I had expected to hear. "Any idea what he planned to do with it?"

Tucker lifted one shoulder. "Not sure really. He said he was working on a project, nothing more, and I'm not one to pry into what my customers are doing unless they ask for help."

Mike said, "If we're talking about what happened last night, it was a dang shame that Malcom had a heart attack. He was quiet but a good guy and a top-notch writer. One time he told me his focus was on investigative journalism, true crime."

I kept my face neutral, hoping Mike would spill a few more details.

He didn't disappoint. "He mentioned he was working

on a big story, one that would cause a few people to go to jail."

"Any idea what paper he was working for?" I kept my voice controlled but this was an excellent lead.

"Not directly but I got the feeling it was a big deal. Ya know, maybe he wrote under an assumed name to keep any disgruntled subjects from finding him. Payback and all."

That got my head spinning with ideas. Maybe he was killed by someone he had exposed; however, before I jumped to any conclusions, I needed to find out where his work had been published and read some articles to get a feel for what he could be writing about this time. True crime topics were, sadly, almost unlimited. Cold cases right up to active investigations. Tucker disappeared into the back without a word, which was odd since that wasn't like him. Before I could follow, he came back to the desk with what looked to be a newspaper article.

Handing it to me, he said, "A couple of months back he gave me this. Said he wrote it. Not that it has a byline or the paper's name, but you might be able to trace it."

I took the article and said, "Thanks." Glancing down, I saw it was about a crime family's corruption and trial. This would be interesting reading and with Dax's connections, it would be pretty straightforward finding out what publication it had been in.

My eyes met Tucker's and it was apparent he was concerned. "I do appreciate this." Had he heard it wasn't a heart attack and was just not saying anything to help my search for the truth?

He gave a curt nod and Mike looked at him. "Malcom was younger than us; we might want to check in with the doc and make sure we're in tip-top shape. I for one wouldn't want some haunted house scare to be the last thing that pushed my ticker to the point of just not ticking."

Mike had such a way with words. Not. "A checkup is always a good idea." I held up the article. "Thanks again for this, Tuck, and if any of you think of anything else, be sure to let me know."

The men reassured me they would and I left with more knowledge than when I went in. On the sidewalk I paused, looking around. I had to chuckle when I realized Tucker's Hardware was like Twisted Scissors Hair Salon on the direct opposite side of the street. Both could offer up juicy tidbits of what was happening around town. I just needed to know what questions to ask to get the conversation rolling.

I jotted off a text asking Dax to meet me at the station. It was important to find out if Malcom was writing under a pen name and was he freelance or did he write for a specific newspaper or magazine? Before I could put my phone in my pocket, he replied by stating he'd be over in about a half hour. Glancing in the direction of the bookstore, I had to wonder if he was still hanging out with Lily. Not that it mattered. Lily and I were dating, and they had become good friends. Besides, he really didn't know many people in town so it made sense. He was at loose ends and if I was in his shoes, I'd want to hang around the bookstore too. It had a good vibe and a beautiful owner.

Whistling, I strolled around the perimeter of the park before heading to the station. With any luck, the report from the medical examiner would be in. Not that I expected to learn more about the gunshot but it was always possible. I would also take another look at the crime scene pictures from the grange hall. There had to be a clue as to who the other clown was, and where did he go?

. . .

Dax entered my office a while later. I glanced at the time and saw it had been exactly a half hour. "How was your research?"

He slumped in my extra chair across from my desk. "I never made it back to the hotel."

"Oh?" I took a sip of lukewarm coffee. With any luck that didn't sound like I had layered more into that question other than mild curiosity.

"I wanted to talk to Lily about this book she keeps saying she's reading. It must be fascinating. I swear she's been reading it since I got here."

Sputtering, I said, "She's an avid reader." I knew exactly which book he was referring to, but it wasn't common knowledge Pembroke Cove had a coven of witches in residence and more importantly, most people would never believe it anyway.

He quirked a brow in my direction. "What's up with her cat, Milo? He sure does meow a lot." With a shrug, he said, "You know, meowing all the time. Is he healthy?"

"He's good and Lily adores him. They have a very special bond." Again, with Milo being a familiar, it was not a casual topic of conversation between non-magical people.

"Does he carry on like that normally when you're around?"

I snorted and tried to cover it up with a laugh. "He's always looking for a treat."

Dax leaned back in the chair and folded his arms over his midsection. "Do you speak cat?"

"I'm more of a dog person myself. Remember I adopted Brutus and I can tell you I don't need to speak dog. That boy has a way of letting me know exactly what he wants, when he wants it."

He nodded. "Animals do have a way about them." Sitting up, he rubbed his hands together in anticipation of our conversation. "What did you find out this morning? I got the idea you discovered an interesting tidbit."

I slid the newspaper article across my desk. "Any chance you can find out where this was published, when, and who has the byline?"

Dax picked it up and scanned the contents. He gave a low whistle. "I remember this case. A family was on trial for a couple of murders and they were trying to influence witnesses and a judge." He gave me a hard look. "I use the word family with a loose interpretation."

"Understood." I gestured to the article. "I got that from Tucker. He said Malcom Sloane gave that to him and Tuck got the impression Malcom wrote true crime articles under a pen name. He'd even said that his next article was going to blow the doors off something big, put people in jail."

"That's a bold statement." Dax continued to study the article. "I know just the person who can find out for us. Give me an hour."

"Sure. You can use the empty office next door to make calls."

Pushing back his chair, Dax stood up. "Thanks, and this article spells out exactly how everything happened. If Malcom wrote this, he had an inside track with a detective. Out of curiosity, have you been talking to anyone lately about any case?"

My heart stuttered in my chest. "The only person I ever talk to is Lily." Could she be in danger over something I was working on? But at the moment nothing was happening.

A mask filtered over Dax's face. "I'll find out as fast as I can. Don't go anywhere without letting me know."

I stood up. "Last I checked I don't report to you."

"It's not about you, Erikson. It's about Lily. She doesn't need to get caught in the cross fire of anything that might be going on, real or conjecture."

Not moving from behind the desk, I said, "I would never do anything to put her in harm's way. You know that. But she has a way of uncovering details which has put her in the crosshairs."

"Then you'd best figure out what happened to our clown before she really starts digging in."

I narrowed my gaze. "What was she doing when you left the store?"

He walked to the door and paused before stepping into the hall. "Not that she said but if I could read her mind, she was planning on going over to Malcom Sloane's place to see what she could find out."

"She wouldn't go over there by herself."

Dax cocked a brow. "If Sloane was killed because of something he was writing about and she discovered any evidence that could lead to that person's identity, either Sloane or the shooter, she could very well get herself into another pickle."

"Then you and I had better find out all we can and fast before she does find herself in a boatload of mischief."

"Or worse." With that comment, he walked away from me.

I knew the investigator was right, but he wasn't aware of her hidden talents which seemed to always help her in unpredictable situations—heck, me too. A couple of months back we had gone out to dinner with William and a large sign came crashing down on top of me. Lily had used a levitation spell to save me from being crushed. If Dax knew, he'd be less concerned but still would worry about what she might inadvertently wander into.

Picking up my cell phone from the desk, I dialed but instead of waiting for it to connect, I hung up. This was more of an in-person conversation. On the way out of my office, I stopped in at Dax's borrowed office.

"I'm headed over to the bookstore, but I won't be gone long."

He gave me a nod of approval. "I scanned the article and one of our IT people is searching now. By the time you're back, I should know something more."

Peabody and Mac were on their way into the station when I got to the lobby.

She asked, "Got a minute? We discovered something near the coffin, you know where we believe our shooter was hiding."

Torn between asking them to wait or going over to Lily's store, I gestured to the vacant conference room to the left of where we stood. "Let's talk in here."

Mac put an evidence bag on the conference table. "This was wedged under one side of the coffin. I think that is how the shooter kept the side propped up. It would have been enough to get fingers in there for quick and effortless access."

Inside was a triangular-shaped pen that had the logo of Teddy Roberts' former real estate agency. I picked up the bag and turned it over. It wasn't cracked and other than a little dirt, it was in good shape. "I wonder whose fingerprints will turn up on the shaft of the pen?"

Peabody took the bag. "It's going to depend if we're dealing with a pro or an amateur, cold and calculated, or a crime of opportunity and passion."

"Valid points. Text me when you've got the results."

"Will do, Detective."

Mac stepped aside so I could walk from the room.

"See if there are still records of clients who Teddy met with during the last couple of months of his life. Hopefully they're easily accessed." To my way of thinking, they'd still be leads to sell a house but who knows how people think.

"Detective?" Peabody said.

I knew where she was going with that single word. "If there is a connection in Teddy's old records, Dax's case just got a breath of new life. Not leaping to conclusions but Malcom might have been investigating something big. His words, not mine. That could be a connection to the real estate fraud. I'm going to say there will be zero prints on that pen and last night's events were an attempt to stop the truth from coming to light."

She nodded. "But little do they know, nothing will stop us from getting justice."

Mac nodded. "Like my dad always said when he'd come off the fishing boat, if it smells like a dead fish, then it's a dead fish."

His comment gave me a momentary chuckle. "Mac, my old friend, this is starting to smell like week-old dead fish." I gestured to the office that Dax was holed up in. "Do me a favor and fill Peters in on what's developed. If this pans out, he's going to be very busy and we'll be working together so let's share our intel."

"Got it, boss." Peabody touched the brim of her service hat with two fingers in a salute.

Now it was time to see what Lily was pondering since she had no idea things just got a lot hotter for the investigation.

Chapter 7
Lily

I got out of my car and approached Malcom Sloane's tidy Cape Cod-style home. The sun was high in the cerulean-blue sky and despite how the day looked deceptively warm, it was downright cold. But the air didn't have the crisp smell of impending snow, at least not yet. The white picket fence outlined the front yard and despite the time of year, it was immaculate, not a stray fallen leaf in sight. I studied his house from the sidewalk, wondering, if he had lived here for the last five years, why didn't I know more about him. It was a shame it took his death for me to stop by his house. Seeing him around town, he had seemed friendly enough, just a bit standoffish.

It was so quiet I could hear myself breathe as I looked up and down the deserted street. Taking several deep breaths, I wondered if I should toss a protection spell around me for this little adventure. But I wasn't even sure if that worked on me or if it was just when I projected it to another. The couple of times I had used it I was able to protect Aunt Mimi and Gage, but I hadn't even thought to ask if it worked on me too. I brushed aside the worry and knew I had other things I could use if I needed magic.

I hurried up the driveway and looked around. What was the easiest route to get around the fence into the backyard? Tucked under a large yew was a gate on the other side of the garage. I eased the latch as it groaned in protest. Surmising it wasn't used often, I crept inside, doing my best to keep the noise to a minimum. Even though the owner wouldn't be coming back, I didn't want a neighbor calling the police and have to explain what I was doing here. Really, this was all due to Victor; he dangled information and I lapped it up the way Milo slurps tuna juice from the can.

The backyard was as tidy as the front. There was a small glass-walled porch overlooking the dormant flower gardens. From this vantage point, I could see a desk littered with papers and a chair pushed back that gave the impression someone had just gotten up. I stuck close to the house as I made my way over to the window. Was it my imagination or could someone just have been sitting there? And I wasn't thinking a ghost either.

Tugging on the handle of the sliding glass door, it glided open with little resistance. I waited, listening for anyone moving around, but the house was silent. I stepped inside and slid the door closed. This room was open to a dining area and an oversized kitchen. What a great layout. Maybe I should think of adding a glass room too, even though it might be impractical during the harsh Maine winters.

Reminding myself I wasn't here to browse for home improvement ideas, I looked at the papers scattered on the desktop. There were handwritten notes of what I guessed were a person's initials, a couple of words after each, and they were a few rows long. The information was cryptic, but I saw:

T.R. met with Mr. $$

Could he be referring to Teddy Roberts? Then it said:

F.G. knows!

But that was crossed out. A chill ran down my spine when it was noted the date of Flora Gray's death.

V.S. Pawn or accomplice?

Now it was starting to make sense. Whatever Malcom had been working on was related to Dax's case of fraud, but how? And if these notes were to be believed, he was investigating Victor Seidel. I pulled out my phone and using a corner of my shirt, I picked up a pen from the desk and began to push papers around and snapped a series of pictures that I could look at more in depth later. Stashing my phone in my inside jacket pocket, I replaced the pen and decided it was time to go deeper into the house.

Leaving the bright sun behind, the interior of the house was gloomy with heavy drapes covering all the windows. I could use my phone as a flashlight but I stopped midstep. With a simple spell I could locate a flashlight and as long as I didn't leave any fingerprints, no one would need to know I had been here, namely Gage.

I stood in the middle of the kitchen. The counters were clear except for a power cord, like the one that went to my laptop. No flashlight. I closed my eyes, focused on an escalator in front of me. This spell was getting easier each time I did it. With a smile, I realized it was like riding a bike. Mentally, I got on and rode to the top, knowing a mini Milo would be waiting for me to ask for what I needed. Once there, I nodded to the kitten, asked for assistance in finding a flashlight, and thanked him before making the return trip down the escalator. It wasn't like fairy dust and the minute I opened my eyes, I would know where to look. It usually took more time than that. But this time, as soon as I stepped from the escalator, I knew to open the bottom drawer of the hutch next to me. Resting inside was a long black heavy-duty flashlight. It made me think of the one Gage carried in his pickup truck. The beam was bright as I fanned the light from side to side. The interior of the house was unlike the desk. Nothing was out of place. It was almost too neat for anyone to have actually lived here. The side tables were empty, not even a trace of dust. I moved down the hall to check out the two bedrooms on this floor. Both were empty and looked to be more storage and guest room type spaces. The primary bedroom had to be upstairs.

I stood at the base of the stairwell, turned off the flashlight, and looked up. A soft groan reached my ears. Was that a floorboard or a person? I hesitated, half torn if I should call Gage. Curiosity propelled me forward. I'd check things out first and then call him.

Glad I had slipped my sneakers on before leaving the store, the soles made little sound. I crept up one stair at a time, pausing after each step, listening for an indication I wasn't alone. But all was quiet. When I reached the next to the last step, I leaned forward, looking right, into one bedroom and then left into the other. One room was dark like the first floor of the house, but the other was bright and sunny. That must be Malcom's room.

I cautiously stepped inside and this was entirely different. Contents of drawers were scattered over the floor; hangers were ripped from the closet; pillows were sliced open and feathers littered the top of the bed; pages of books were ripped out and strewn about willy-nilly.

I took a step away from the door and as I said, "What the heck happened in here?" the door creaked behind me.

"Lily. Lily. Open your eyes."

I could hear Gage and the shakiness in his voice, his finger stroking my cheek. "Sweetheart, open your eyes."

"Is she bleeding?"

Was that Dax? I tried to force my eyes open and I could see slits of light. "What?"

"Shush, it's okay now. You're safe."

I tried to sit up and a searing pain filled the back of my head. "Where are we?"

Gage slid an arm around my shoulders and supported me while I got into a full sitting position. "Malcom Sloane's house. His bedroom to be exact."

It came flooding back to me. "I was looking around on the first floor and I heard what sounded like a groan. I came upstairs and found his bedroom had been ransacked."

It was then I noticed the room was as neat as a pin. As if a magic wand had erased the mess. I looked at Gage, worry etched into his face. "It was a disaster, clothes all over the floor, books ripped apart, feathers from pillows scattered everywhere. Just a mess."

"I believe you." With Gage on one side and Dax on the other, they pulled me to a standing position and my legs wobbled like cooked spaghetti. "Take a deep breath and we can go downstairs."

"When did you get here and how did you know I was here?"

"Questions will be answered once we get you down the stairs and sitting in a chair, okay?"

I nodded and took a shaky step. "Can you call Aunt Mimi and see if she can meet me at home? I've got a major headache and I'm sure she can help."

"I'll call her," Dax said. "Gage, you can walk in front of Lily down the stairs, just in case."

Gage held my hand and arm and was one step ahead of me as Dax gripped the back of my jacket. We moved down the stairs at a snail's pace, one head pounding step at a time. But I was comforted to know I wouldn't fall, that either Gage would catch me or Dax would stop me. Once we reached the bottom, Sharon and Mac were taking pictures and there was the forensics kit open on the floor.

She took a step in my direction. "Hey, Lily. How are you doing? Gage radioed down you'd been hit on the back of the head."

I looked through the house and out the glass door. The sun was sitting lower in the sky and was barely visible over the pine trees in the next yard. I looked at Gage. "I got here around two thirty. What time is it?"

"It's close to four." He glanced at Dax.

"I looked around down here, poked around the papers on the desk and—"

"What desk and papers?" Dax stepped closer to me.

"Out there." I pointed to the wooden desk. My heart rate skipped up. The desk had a folder in the middle, all nice and neat. There was nothing scattered about. "Wait just a minute. That desk was covered with handwritten notes and papers. My guess it was research for whatever Malcom had been working on." I looked at Gage. "Did Sharon or Mac clean it up?"

She took a step toward me. "We haven't processed that room yet, Lily, we wouldn't clean up. It has to stay in the exact same state we find it until we're done with our investigation."

"That's not possible." I looked around and my head began to swim. "I need to sit down."

Mac pulled over a wooden chair and I gave him a grateful nod. "Thank you."

I dropped my head in my hands and Gage rubbed my shoulders. "Take your time and when you're ready, tell me everything that happened from the time you got here."

Still holding my head, I asked, "Dax, did you call my aunt?"

He knelt down next to me. "I did and she said she'd be there waiting for you."

"I'm going to take you home, Lily, and we can talk about everything after Mimi fixes you some tea."

"Gage, I think Lily should go to the emergency room. She needs more than a cup of tea brewed by her aunt." The deep Southern drawl had all but disappeared from Dax's voice and even if he didn't know it, Aunt Mimi was exactly who I needed. She could heal me better than the doctor could.

"Mimi works with natural remedies that Lily responds well to. And if that is what Lily wants to do, then I'll support her."

I knew that authoritative tone of Gage's voice too. I lifted my head. "Stop it, both of you. I make my own decisions." Looking at Dax, I said, "My aunt will take care of me and if I feel I need to go to the hospital later, I will." Next my gaze leveled on Gage. "I'll tell my story once here, and then if you have questions, you can ask me later." No one should mistake the steel in my voice now. "Do I make myself clear?"

"Like a crystal ball," Dax said, still kneeling beside me.

The irony of his statement didn't fall short for me or Gage based on the way amusement flicked through his eyes.

"If anyone wants to take notes, now would be the time to start."

Gage said, "Go ahead, Lily."

"I got here like I said sometime around two thirty. Aunt Mimi was late to the store, and I had to wait for her before I could leave. Once I got here, I looked around in the front and backyard and noticed it was very quiet. One of the glass doors was unlocked so I came inside and the first thing I noticed were the papers covering Malcom's desk. He was laying out his clues with initials and a few additional words on each line." I looked around. "Where's my bag?"

"I didn't see it; did you leave it in your car?"

Relief washed over me. "Right. It's in the trunk." I dug my phone out of the inside pocket of my coat, relieved it was still there. "I took pictures of most of the pages, and I can pull them up on the computer when we get back to my place, but he mentioned TR, FG, and VS. I think he was referring to Teddy Roberts, Flora Gray, and Victor Seidel. This case has to be tied into Dax's case."

Dax shook his head. "And this means that you put yourself in a killer's scope."

I flicked my hand, brushing off his concern. "No. What this means is we have a clear connection between your investigation and two of the last three murders in Pembroke Cove." I couldn't help but grin and do a small victorious fist pump in the air. While Gage and Dax had been trolling for clues, I had discovered the real connection. Score one for the witch.

"Don't get too excited. Since there seems to be a link between what had happened in the past and now this new crime, you need to stay out of it and let Dax take the lead. Our police department will back him up as needed."

Dax nodded as Gage was talking and I glared at both of them. "If it wasn't for me, you wouldn't have put this together as quickly. It's because you came looking for me that you realized it, and if I hadn't gotten the pictures of those papers, you'd have very little or zero evidence to connect the dots."

Gage started to shake his head and I held up my index finger, warning him to stop before he said something that would lead us down the road to an argument.

"You can thank me later. But what took you so long to find me?"

"The medical examiner called in his report and Dax got a call back from his office."

"And?" I couldn't believe I had to pry this out of either of them.

"Malcom Sloane died from a single gunshot wound to the heart. Dax dug into Malcom's background and he is a well-respected journalist under the pen name of M. S. Sloane. Which confirms our suspicion that he was writing an article on what has been happening in town. By the time we reviewed the new information, Mimi called and said she expected you back from your quest for clues and you weren't answering your cell."

Dax said, "That's when we put two and two together and figured you'd come here."

I stood up and swayed before steadying myself with a hand on the back of the chair. "Two heads are better than one in this case. Now who's going to drive me home? I have a witch to see about a headache."

Chapter 8
Lily

Aunt Mimi's car was in my driveway when Dax parked my car. The minute I got out, Gage was at my elbow with Dax on the other side. I'm sure they were giving me the appearance of a frail old woman when all I got was knocked on the head. No big deal.

The back door opened and Aunt Mimi came out, her arms open wide, and Nate was behind her. For a brief second, I wondered why he wasn't on his lobster boat but that didn't matter. All I wanted was to have her arms wrapped around me.

I heard Dax say to Gage, "Why did she call her aunt a witch?"

I didn't turn around, confident Gage could handle it.

"Aunt Mimi." Tears pricked my eyes.

"My dear niece." Her arms held me tight and she began whispering words I didn't understand but I didn't care. I was safe.

Nate told the guys to come inside and the door closed softly, leaving me and my aunt on the deck. She continued to speak softly, holding me close. Then she relaxed her arms, opening them wider. She tipped her head back with her eyes closed. I wasn't sure if I was to do the same. I eased my head back as far as it would go without pain and closed my eyes, but my arms felt like lead weights so I turned my palms skyward. I took several long, deep cleansing breaths.

Aunt Mimi touched my hand. "We should go in so I can look at your head."

I reached back and my fingers grazed an egg-sized lump. But nothing felt sticky. "It's not so bad."

She cupped my cheek with her hand. "You were very lucky this time, but the next time, please put a protection spell around you and wear it like a cloak."

"I can do that?" I could feel my eyes widen as she smiled.

"I take it the book hasn't shown you that particular spell. For some reason that book is only giving you what it deems useful."

"No." I didn't shake my head to keep any residual pain at bay. "I was thinking of the one I used for you and Gage."

"The personal spell is different. Later, ask the book to reveal it and if it doesn't, I'll teach you." She opened the door. "Park your behind in a kitchen chair and I'll make a healing tea."

"Don't forget we have company so if you want to cast a spell..." My words fizzled out. "That's what you were doing when you were hugging me."

"And then I gave thanks for bringing you safely home to me." Her soft-brown eyes were clouded. "I thought you promised Gage no more solo investigating."

Stuffing my hands in my jacket pocket, my fingers grazed my phone. "In my defense, I never thought it could be dangerous in broad daylight. Don't bad guys know the rules and come out after dark?"

Shaking her head, she said, "Only you would expect criminals to follow some sort of rules." She opened the door. "Inside with you."

The conversation died as we entered and Gage reached me in a couple of long strides. Questions lingered in his eyes.

I took his hand. "I'm okay. Aunt Mimi is going to make some tea and the fresh air helped."

The door banged closed and I winced at the sound. Obviously, the spell hadn't worked like magic. "I need to sit."

Dax pulled out a chair at the table and Gage held my hand as I eased down. Four pairs of eyes watched me. I gestured to the empty chairs. "Sit. I feel like an exhibit at the zoo with you all staring at me." I placed my phone on the table. "But first can someone get my laptop so we can look at these pictures I took of Malcom's desk?"

Nate said, "Is it in your office, Lily?"

"No, it should be on my nightstand." He walked down the hall and Gage got up.

"Are you going to want your clue board too?"

I nodded.

Dax looked perplexed. "You got bonked over the head and were unconscious for over an hour. Now we're going to have tea and look at clues? You should go to the hospital and get scans or something."

That was such a non-magical thing to say, and I looked to Aunt Mimi for help. How were we going to get out of this? I was beginning to feel better; whatever incantation she had used was working.

Aunt Mimi's eyes glinted and she said, "If I thought Lily needed a medical doctor, I would insist upon it, but in our family, we have certain talents and one of mine is the gift of healing which has been passed down through the generations." She crossed the room and placed a hand on his shoulder. Looking him in the eye, she said, "Don't worry, I promise you Lily is healing as she sits there and the tea I'm going to brew has ingredients that have been used for generations. She will fully recover." She glanced my way. "Well, with the exception of her rushing into situations before considering the consequences."

Dax's face relaxed and his shoulders lost their tension. I had to wonder if under my aunt's touch, a spell was woven around him to accept our truth.

He looked at me and then at my aunt. "Mimi, if you say it is so, then so it shall be."

Aunt Mimi's eyes locked on mine. I replayed his last comment. It sounded almost like a spell. I tipped my head and gave her a questioning look and she blinked, indicating she had heard it too. It was the look we used when playing cards against Nate and Gage.

"Here's your computer." Nate set it on the table in front of me and looked at his bride. "What's going on in here?"

"Not a thing. I need to get the tea brewed." She removed her hand from Dax's shoulder and then, as if it was the most natural thing in the world, she said, "Nate, would you like to help me prepare dinner while Lily shares what she learned with Gage and Dax?"

Gage came out of the closet holding the clue board. "I could not get this thing to budge. It was like it was glued to the floor or something."

"Well, Gage, you were successful." She gave me a wink.

Someday I hoped I'd be her kind of witch, little spells happening simultaneously. Instead of my sole focus on one at a time.

"Now, tea first and then dinner. I'm sure you're all

starving. Police work is draining." With that she pointed at the kettle and it floated to the sink to be filled. I stole a look at Dax, but he seemed to be completely oblivious to the odd happenings.

I sent the pictures from my phone to my laptop. After a couple of clicks they filled the screen, layered one on top of the other until the first picture I took was full size.

"As you can see, the desk was covered with papers." I turned the computer around so Gage and Dax could take a look. "The next image is of the list I was telling you about. See the TR, FG, and VS notations? This does indicate he was investigating the real estate shenanigans that have been swirling around Pembroke Cove."

Dax pulled the screen closer and nodded. "I wonder who he thought Mr. Dollar Sign was." He tapped the next button and continued to scroll through the pictures. Gage had pulled his chair closer so he could watch and I was left looking through the images on my phone. So much for me making an important connection to the murder case and now basically being excluded. I stood and held on to the back of the chair, waiting to make sure my head wasn't going to spin again. It was clear, with just a twinge of pain in the back. Nate handed me an ice pack he had just pulled from the freezer, wrapped in a tea towel.

"This is for the swelling."

I said, "Thanks," and brought the chalkboard closer to my chair. Then I took the ice pack before sitting down. Now I could make notes and tend the egg on the back of my head at the same time.

I wrote *Malcom Sloane Victim* across the top with a line down the middle. *Suspect* was the header in the left column and in the right *Motive*.

The first suspects listed were Mr. Money Bags as I called him, Victor Seidel, and the shooter.

SuspectMotive

Mr. $$Loss of Money
Victor Seidel ??
ShooterDiscovery
Other ClownWho are you?

Dax grinned. He nodded in the direction of the clue board. Gage also looked at the board.

"This is how she works. Every time she learns something new, she creates a new board, but she has already taken a picture of the previous version. At some point she might print them out and place them side by side." He leaned the chair back on two legs and a look of pride filled his face. "This is how she processes a puzzle."

"Lily, you have a mind for police work. I think you missed your true calling," Dax said.

"No, this is for fun. If I was in law enforcement, I wouldn't have time to spend with Milo or read all the books I want." I glanced around. "Where is my furry best friend?"

As if he was waiting for his cue, the kitty door pushed open and he stalked in, glancing at me and then the rest of the group.

He paused and gave me his version of an annoyed glare. "Did you forget about me at the bookstore?" Looking at Dax and Gage and then my aunt and Nate, he grumbled, "What happened now?"

I got up and scooped him into my arms. Nuzzling the top of his head, I said, "I'm going to take Milo in the other room so he doesn't trip anyone up making dinner." As I hurried from the room, I noticed Dax's eyes were wide and he had questions lingering there. Was it the way I had reacted when Milo walked in? He couldn't understand my familiar talking to me, could he? I pushed the thought aside and entered my bedroom, closing the door behind me.

I set him on the bed and lay down next to him. "I'm sorry, Milo. You know I went over to Malcom Sloane's house and while I was poking around, I got hit over the head."

He stood on his back legs and placed his paws on my arm. "Are you hurt?"

"I was out cold for a while, but Aunt Mimi did some healing stuff and I'm better. I'm surprised you didn't sense I was in trouble."

"My dear witch..." He stalked around my head to take a closer look. "We are connected and if the situation were dire, I might know but our familiar to witch bond hasn't gotten as strong as it will. We've only been actively bonding on this level for a few months. Something like that takes years."

Tears pricked my eyes. "You do care I got hurt?"

He jumped into my lap and patted my cheek with his soft paw. "Of course I do. You're my person."

I started to cry. The events of the day were a lot but Milo being sweet was overwhelming.

"After all, I'm just starting to break you in. I'd hate to have to start all over with a new witch. It can be exhausting." He yawned. "You should dry your eyes and get back out to Detective Cutie. We can talk later and tonight you're going to read that book and learn the self-protection spell."

I groaned. "Will you ever stop nagging about reading *Practical Beginnings*?"

"Not until you're an accomplished witch and at the rate you're actually putting the work in, well, let's just say we both might have gone to the great coven in the sky before you actually do finish reading it."

I got up from the bed and stamped my foot with fake irritation. He was right, I just didn't want to admit it. "Fine. Tonight, we'll read the book together."

Milo landed on the floor with a soft thud. He swished his tail and gave me a long look. "I've already read it."

Flinging my hands wide, I asked, "Then why don't you teach me all the important stuff now and save me the trouble?"

"That would be like giving you a driver's license without taking driver's education. You'd be a menace on the roads. And that is not the kind of familiar you want to have. There will be no shortcuts on my shift."

"One of these days you're going to do something to make learning all my spells easy for me."

"There is no way to circumvent being a great witch, and you, Lily Michaels, are destined to be one of the best."

He stalked from the room and my mouth dropped open. Did he just give me a future compliment?

"Lily?" Gage called. "Your tea is getting cold."

"Coming." I grabbed a tissue and dried my cheeks and dabbed my eyes. No sense letting everyone know I had been crying. Dax would insist on taking me to the emergency room.

When I got back to the table, next to Malcom's name on the board was a dash, freelance reporter.

"We already knew that about Malcom. Wasn't it more important who was going to publish the article?"

Dax grinned. "It was going national. My contact at the office said all the biggest news outlets were waiting for it but the story would be breaking news in *The Post*."

I was confused. That didn't seem like the best way to get this information to the world.

Dax snapped his fingers. "I know that look and you're asking why *The Post*? Am I right?"

I sat down and sipped my tea, waiting for him to answer the rhetorical question. When he didn't elaborate, I said, "Yes. Why that paper?"

"Mafia news is always published there first. So, Malcom must believe Mr. Money Bags is part of a crime family." He leaned back in his chair with a wide grin as if he had just discovered the secret to life.

"And this is news to who?" I couldn't believe a federal investigator wouldn't have already come to that conclusion. "And if a crime family is involved, why would they have shot Malcom at the haunted house? At a family event. Aren't people who are in that line of work typically protective of innocents?"

Dax said, "Not always. Sometimes it's about the opportunity and lack of a chance to be discovered."

I sipped my tea again. "You're suggesting that a professional hit man snuck into town, somehow got involved in our little haunted house, dug out a space under the coffin, hid there and waited until Malcom, dressed in a clown costume, came along and just happened to get shot?"

"Yes."

"Dax, what about the other clown? If what you're suggesting is probable, there could have been another shooting where the wrong clown was the victim."

I got up and took the chalk, circling the clown in my suspect list. I spun around. "I have another theory."

Gage arched his brow and leaned forward. "Are you suggesting the other clown either could have been the target or was the shooter?"

Dax looked from me to Gage. "It might be a bit far-fetched but possible."

I grinned. "I'm going out on a broom here; the other clown was the target and for some reason Malcom showed up, maybe meeting the other clown for information about his story. And maybe the other clown knew of the potential danger and used Malcom as a decoy to escape."

I slapped my hand on the table. "That's it. Figuring out the other clown's identity is key and I believe Victor can help us."

Chapter 9
Gage

I was struck by how far Lily's mind jumped to the conclusion that Victor might have answers about the other clown. Before I knew it, I was suggesting she go with me to talk to him. Now it was early the next morning and I was sitting in her driveway second-guessing my brilliant idea. The last thing I wanted was to keep her in the line of fire.

She came out the door and twisted the knob, making sure it was locked, but I didn't see Milo. After she got in and buckled up, I asked, "Where's your little bundle of fur?"

She looked out the side window as if she might see him before answering. "I'm not sure. He was already gone when I got up." With a frown, she locked her gaze on me. "He was pretty upset about yesterday and me getting into a tight spot. We worked on a self-protection spell last night until I perfected it. Maybe he was just tired when he left this morning and needed a break from me."

I clasped her hand. "How's your head now?"

She reached back and touched the spot where a large egg shape yesterday had protruded from under her short chestnut hair. "It's fine. Aunt Mimi's got the magic touch." She gave me a small smile. "Pun intended."

"Indeed, she does. Mom said many of the witches in town go to her when they need a potion for healing."

The smile reached her sable-brown eyes. "I'm glad everyone knows she's amazing."

Starting the car, I backed out of the driveway. "Are you sure you're up to talking with Victor?"

The smile that appeared on her lips said it all; she was excited to be a part of the conversation. "Yes. Don't you find it curious that he's been in town for a while and we just discover he's into real estate development? What are the chances he's Mr. Dollar Sign guy?"

Driving through town, I kept my eyes peeled for anything amiss. But all was normal for Main Street. "Slim. It's just too easy and investigations are never that straight-forward. He could be a legitimate businessman enjoying the slower pace of life in Maine in between work trips."

"Have you been to his house before today?"

I slowed and took a left out of town headed out on Route One. "No, but Peabody was telling me about it this morning when I stopped at the station. It's a log cabin with tons of glass, not a typical oceanfront home which around here is more along the lines of a Victorian cottage. This place is more suited to a mountain retreat."

"But he has an ocean view? Very interesting."

The rest of the drive slipped by as we rode in compan-ionable silence. I glanced at Lily a few times and she was chewing on her bottom lip, which meant her mind was whirling.

I drove down the narrow two-lane road. On one side we could see the ocean in the distance and the other side were smaller summer homes closed for the season. At the end of the access road, it would fan out north and south to follow the beach lined with houses that had weathered many years here, perched on the rocky coast. Up ahead I saw the wrought iron fence line which opened up to a blacktop driveway. Most houses around here left the entrance in its natural stone and seashell state. But the house oozed money. "By the looks of this property, it seems Victor does very well in business."

Lily was taking in every detail as we pulled up to the house built on top of the bluff. "Peabody was right about the log cabin but it also has the local vibe with the cedar shake siding in some areas." She got out of the car and snapped her collar up on her jacket. "The breeze is brisk."

"That's early November on the bluff." Victor was walking in our direction with a wide smile, waving. "Good morning, Detective, Lily. Welcome to my home. I wish it had been under different circumstances." His smile dimmed as he came back to the reason for our visit. "Please come inside. I have coffee ready."

Victor opened up the side door and ushered Lily in first and I was right behind her. We entered a spacious kitchen that flowed into a dining and living space, all facing the water. The views were spectacular. The Atlantic Ocean spilled out before us. Gray-blue waves crashed against the rocky coastline that met the long lush grass. He gestured to the living area with two long sofas and several overstuffed chairs.

"Make yourself comfortable. I'll get the coffee."

We watched as he filled a carafe and placed it, along with mugs, a creamer, and sugar bowl on a tray.

"Did you build the house?" Lily asked.

"It was under construction when I discovered it. I

believe the previous owners ran out of money. I picked it up for a song."

She shot me a sharp look. "Who was your real estate agent?"

"Teddy Roberts handled everything. I came up here looking for an escape and rented a house a few doors down. He was the agent for that too. I fell in love with the location and when he mentioned this place would be going on the market, I made a cash offer and gave Teddy a small bonus for giving me the heads-up. It all worked out."

Had he just admitted to being part of an ongoing investigation? "When did you say that was?" I took the coffee cup he offered me and handed it to Lily.

"Two years ago, August. But then it took another year to rework the design, finish construction, and move in. Of course, I'm only here part-time until I retire." He chuckled. "Sadly, that's twenty years down the road."

Lily added a dash of cream to her coffee and sipped. "What made you come to Pembroke Cove in the first place? We're not exactly the first town people think about relocating to; it's usually a seaside town below Portland."

"My mother had been here a few years back and suggested I check it out. I'd just finished a particularly difficult project and needed to unplug. In fact, she introduced me to Teddy." He looked around like a king surveying his kingdom. "And here I am, happier than I've ever been, anywhere."

I wondered if Victor would keep talking or if I should ask a couple of questions to keep the conversation moving. Before I could, he set his mug on the table next to him and leaned forward, his hands clasped.

"Have you learned what happened to poor Malcom? I had the pleasure of talking to him a few times when we bumped into each other in town. We even had coffee at The Copper Kettle. He seemed like a good egg. Why anyone would want to kill him is just unthinkable."

"We're looking into everything. Did you know him well?"

"Two outsiders trying to find their place in a tight-knit community, let's just say we understood each other." Victor looked out the front window. "No one deserves to be taken out like that and in front of those poor little kids. How's the young Valentine girl?"

Lily said, "Her father shielded her from the worst of it, but she said something interesting. Did you happen to notice there were two clowns walking around?"

He focused on Lily. "Now that you mention it, there were two dressed identically except one was a very skinny clown; the outfit bagged on him."

This was a good observation. "Any idea who the skinny clown might be?"

"The lucky one who walked away." He shrugged. "Sorry for being crass, but I tell it like I see it. Also, the other clown seemed to have a limp, like a stone in the shoe kind of walk."

I nodded. That was the first we had heard that tidbit from anyone and that included Kevin Valentine. But maybe he wasn't the kind of guy to take in small details. Victor hadn't had much to do other than stand around looking at people, waiting for his big moment, popping out of the coffin later in the evening.

I noticed Lily sat up straighter on the sofa and wasn't sure what that was all about, but she must have remembered something. A door closed in the house and instantly I was on alert. As far as I knew Victor lived alone.

He looked in the direction of the noise and said,

"Excuse me for a moment." He hurried down the hall and out of sight.

I whispered to Lily, "What do you think is going on?"

"I'm not sure, but I just thought of something. Malcom's laptop wasn't anywhere in the house."

Of course, with the excitement of finding Lily on the floor, I had overlooked that very important detail. We could talk about it later.

Voices drifted in our direction, and I stood, ready for what, I wasn't sure. Victor was talking to a woman and when they came into view. I noticed she had long gray hair, ice-blue eyes, and was tall and slender. The polite smile on her face didn't reach her eyes.

She crossed the room and extended her hand. "Please forgive me. My son didn't tell me he had company or I would have been here to greet you. I'm Vonni Seidel."

Her grip was firm and her hands, like her eyes, were cool. She then shook Lily's hand. "You're the woman who runs the bookstore in town. Victor said I must stop in, that you have an amazing selection."

"Lily Michaels, and yes, please drop by. If there is a book you want and I don't carry it, I'd be happy to order it for you."

She gestured to where we had been sitting. "Please relax. Victor tells me you've been discussing the incident from the other night at the Halloween event. Tragic. I can't imagine why anyone would choose to commit a crime in front of innocent children."

Lily nodded. "We all agree and we're hopeful Gage will solve the murder quickly." She looked at me and I wasn't sure what she was up to, but whatever she said next, she had my full support.

"In fact, Victor, I was hoping you would consider

joining us when we hold the do-over Halloween on Saturday night. It's a great fundraiser for our other holiday events so it would be a shame to miss out."

"Absolutely, whatever you need," he nodded.

"Good. I was hoping we could count on you."

"But there is one thing."

"Oh, what might that be?" Lily asked.

He visibly paled. "Can we make sure the only part of my coffin that moves is the lid? I wouldn't want anyone hiding under it again. I might actually have a heart attack."

I crossed one leg over my knee. "Speaking of which, do you have any idea who might have made the modifications to the scene?"

He shook his head. "I don't. I'm all thumbs in the home improvement department."

Vonni patted his knee. "He won't even use a screwdriver. When I'm around, I'll hang pictures for him; otherwise, he hires a handyman."

"Who do you use?" Lily asked. "I've been meaning to find someone to do some work at the bookstore."

"Corbin Marks. He's good and fairly priced. I'd highly recommend him. And I was thinking"—he glanced at me— "if it's okay with you, could he go in and fix the coffin back to the way it should be?"

"I'll let you know as soon as we release the grange hall." The reopening of the haunted house had caught me off guard and this was the best response I had on short notice.

"Thanks, I appreciate that. It will help me focus on my role as Victor the vampire, if I don't have to wonder if someone is hiding beneath me."

That was another thread I needed to tug, who had built it originally.

Lily held her coffee cup to her lips and she glanced at

Victor over the rim. "Did you go down to the hall after we closed up for the night to drop off more candy?"

His brow wrinkled. "No. I brought it all with me when I was there earlier in the day. Why?"

Lily said, "It's nothing. Someone just dropped some off and I wasn't sure where it came from."

But she never had a casual comment. Once we got in the car, she'd have a few questions of her own to answer. "Tell me, Mrs. Seidel, are you going to become a full-time resident of Pembroke Cove?"

"Please call me Vonni." There was that practiced smile again. "I have a home in Boston, but I like to escape from time to time. Maine has a slower pace, and then there is the added bonus of my son living here. I'm not sure why when he has a business to run like I do, since it's not as convenient."

"And do you and Victor work for the same company?"

She gave her son an indulgent smile. "No, my son wanted to make his own mark in the real estate business, so after his father passed"—she looked up at the ceiling and blew a kiss—"I took over our family enterprise and Victor developed his own."

"Do you have other children who work with you?"

"I have some nephews who are involved, but my daughter is a surgeon. She wanted nothing to do with the family business." She looked at her watch and got up from the sofa. "Now if you will excuse me, I have a conference call in ten minutes." She shook our hands again before leaving the room.

Lily said as Vonni reached the hallway, "It was a pleasure to meet you."

She fluttered her fingers over her head. "Likewise." And a door closed somewhere down the hall.

Victor cleared his throat. "Mom is always busy with work. She keeps hoping to have grandchildren that will want to run the company someday."

Lily asked, "And what does your mother do?"

He said, "She's in construction."

Chapter 10
Lily

I couldn't wait to get Gage in the car and out of Victor's driveway. There was so much to unpack from our visit. Turning in my seat as far as my seat belt would allow, I said, "Can you believe that? Vonni Seidel is in construction which is a kissing cousin to real estate, and she was the one who hooked him up with Teddy. That can't be a coincidence."

Gage's hand tightened on the steering wheel. "That is interesting, but Victor hasn't mentioned anything about being involved in local real estate. When I checked him out, he's been focused on luxury resorts in exotic locations and a few major shopping malls on the West Coast. The destinations are nothing like our neck of the woods, no matter how beautiful it is. All of his resorts are year-round destinations, not four months of the year."

I slumped in my seat, some of the wind evaporated from my sail. Snapping my fingers, I said, "We need to track down Corbin Marks. He volunteered to help build scenes for the haunted house. His opinion on how long it would have taken for someone to sneak into the grange and change the coffin could be helpful. Or we need to rule out he didn't do it himself."

"I'll make some calls to see if I can find out where he's working today."

I had to tell Gage about the grange hall being open when I got there. It had slipped my mind with all that had happened, and until I thought of the candy idea and Victor, I had tucked it away.

"There is something I forgot to mention about that night."

Gage slowed the car and looked at me. "The tone in your voice leads me to be concerned."

"In my defense there was a lot going on when we discovered Malcom was shot and Josie Valentine had been so close to everything. It slipped my mind until we were talking to Victor."

There was a turnout spot up ahead and Gage pulled in and parked. "Go on."

"When I got to the grange hall before everyone else, the front door was ajar. I went in and checked out all the displays, hoping nothing had been damaged overnight since I assumed I hadn't latched it securely when we closed up. But now, I wonder if whoever altered the coffin snuck back and he was the one who didn't shut the door tight."

He looked out the windshield before speaking. "And you didn't see or hear anything when you went inside?"

"Nope. Everything looked as it should and it was quiet like a tomb." I touched his arm. "I'm sorry I forgot to mention it."

"I get it. We were opening up and nothing was out of place so why not wait to tell me and then the shooting, interviewing everyone, and trying to find out what was going on was information overload. Is there anything else you can think of that I should know?"

"You're up to speed."

He gave me a smile that caused my heart to ramp up. "And I think you're right. Whoever modified the coffin snuck in and left the door cracked. Possibly they were going to come back and hide before we opened. It's hard to tell, but I'm glad you didn't catch anyone in the act."

I hadn't thought of that possibility. A shiver ran down my spine at what might have happened had our suspect been interrupted. "Me too and in the future, I'm going to make sure that door is secured."

Gage put the car in gear and pulled back onto the road. "Where to next?"

There were so many ideas and unanswered questions bouncing around in my head. "I'm not sure. We need to talk to Corbin, Kevin, and Josie Valentine about the second clown, and what about Malcom's laptop? And I didn't have a chance to check and see if there was a sheet of plywood at his house."

"What are you talking about?"

"Tucker said he'd bought one in the last few days." I pulled out my cell and began to scroll through the pictures I had taken at the house. "There was a power cord on the counter but no laptop. Could the person who hit me have taken it, or did Malcom put it someplace he considered safe?"

"Sloane's car was in the parking area and we had it towed to our lot. Peabody inventoried what was inside, not that there was much—an empty coffee cup and a candy bar wrapper—but his laptop was in the trunk. In light of everything, I would say he was keeping it safe."

"Smart guy. Too bad he didn't realize just how much danger lurked."

After driving for a few minutes in silence, I said, "Can you drop me at my bookstore? I'm going to give Kevin Valentine a call to see if I can talk with Josie when she gets out of school."

Gage cleared his throat. "I think that's a job for an actual police officer."

"Well, I figured you'd be there too." I flashed him a quick grin, not that I had given that a thought to begin with, but it was a good idea.

He shook his head. "You are incorrigible, and I'll be happy to meet you at the store and we can walk over to the antique shop together. Also, by then, I'll have an answer about the plywood at Sloane's house."

"It's a date." I was missing my clue board at the moment. There were ideas that just couldn't gel in my brain. But when I got to the store, I'd write down some of the threads that kept appearing, then slipping away. It was possible the clonk on my head was causing my lingering fuzziness.

"What did you think about Victor stating that one of the clowns was skinny? I'm thinking it might have been a woman." Gage slowed the car and stopped in front of my store.

The open sign was visible, and Milo was perched in the front window as if he was waiting for me to arrive. "That is a strong possibility, but something about that clown bugs me." Pushing open the door, I said, "It will come to me." I leaned over and gave Gage a quick kiss on the lips. "I'll see you around three? With any luck, we can get this wrapped up today with Josie."

"I have a few leads to track down too and I'm going to

ask Dax to join us when we stop by Kevin's store. Since this is tied back to his case, he needs to be included."

"You're right. See you later." I closed the car door and walked behind it, totally lost in putting order to the clues in front of me. The door opened and I almost ran into it as Nikki came out.

"Well, hey there. I had almost given up hope that you'd show up. Your aunt didn't know when you were going to come in."

I gave her a quick squeeze. "If you had told me you were going to stop in this morning, I could have tried to get here sooner."

Nikki followed me inside. I stopped to give Milo a quick kiss on the head and whispered, "Stick around. I have some information to bounce off you."

"Of course you do." He did a lazy stretch and then proceeded to curl into a ball on his window seat cushion.

"What brings you by?" I hung up my jacket and pointed at the coffee pot to turn it on. It was time I started using my magic for little things. It was a muscle I needed to exercise to make it stronger.

Aunt Mimi's eyes opened wide, beaming. "Well done."

I winked at her. "I'm learning."

Nikki opened a bakery box that was on the counter. "I made some pumpkin scones this morning."

Now she was beating around the bush. What did she need to talk about? "Are we all having coffee or should I brew tea?"

My aunt picked up her jacket. "I need to run, but I'll be around if you need me to cover the store later." She fluttered her fingers in a brief wave as she closed the door. Her hasty exit didn't give me a chance to even thank her for taking care of the store.

"I'll have coffee." Nikki placed a scone on a deep-purple paper plate she had also brought.

Now I was getting nervous with the way she was setting up the small table. But she wasn't going to talk until she was good and ready. "I'll just get our mugs."

With coffee brewed, I fixed ours the way we drank them, then I joined her near the front of the shop. Nikki was looking out the window, definitely distracted.

"Here's your coffee." She glanced up and took the mug that said *I'm booked for the weekend.*

"Thank you." Taking a sip, she gave me a weak smile.

"Okay, what is going on? I can't remember when I've seen you so glum and you should be walking on cloud nine being engaged to Steve."

"Do you think we're rushing into marriage?" Her large baby blue eyes had pricks of tears lingering in them.

"Not at all. You two remind me of the ocean and the sand, forever connected."

"You think so? We got into a huge fight this morning over when we should have the wedding. I want a summer wedding and Steve wants to get married at Christmas, like in less than six weeks. I tried to tell him there isn't enough time to plan a wedding, but he said we didn't need to make a big deal about it. Invite a few friends, our family, and stand in front of the preacher. We could tie the knot in our living room and that would be it."

Now I understood. Steve was trying to express his desire to get their future started and it didn't matter what kind of a wedding they had as long as they had each other. And I was sure Nikki, like me, had been dreaming of her wedding after the first time we married off our Barbies to the Ken and GI Joe dolls.

I leaned over and took her hands in mine. "How did you and Steve leave it this morning?"

Nikki's eyes were glued to the floor. "I told him if he couldn't understand how important the wedding was, then maybe we shouldn't bother to get married at all."

An idea popped in my mind. "What if you compromised on the wedding date? We could plan a Valentine's Day wedding. It will be almost halfway between what you both want and that gives us plenty of time to plan the best day of your life."

She lifted her face and with a tentative smile asked, "Do you think we can?"

"I know we can and when you present this idea to Steve, tell him marriage is about compromise and this is your first one and not the last." I got up. "Wait here."

I walked into the office and pulled a brown paper bag from the shelf. This would put that smile back on her face. "Take a look. I was planning on giving this to you on Friday night when we go out to dinner and celebrate, but I think it's better you have it now."

Nikki opened the bag and slid out four magazines. Her eyes grew bright, and a grin filled her face. "Bridal magazines."

"Since you asked me to be your maid of honor, I take my duties very serious and this is just the beginning. I thought we could take a trip to Boston and look for your dress with our moms and Steve's too if she can join us. We'll make a weekend of it."

She jumped up from the chair and threw her arms around my neck. "Thank you, Lily. You are the best maid of honor and friend any girl could have."

"Now, you need to head over to the garage and talk to

Steve. Get the date worked out. Once that's all set, we can start planning."

"I'm leaving right now." With one final hug, she hurried out the back door and I was sure there would be nothing but happy tears from this point forward for my best friends.

G age was coming to the shop so that we could walk to Kevin's store together. While waiting, I added a few more details to my substitute clue board.

Milo was sitting on the countertop watching me. "What are you thinking?"

I tapped my pencil on the sketch I had drawn of the grange hall. "If someone was waiting in that space under the coffin to shoot Malcom, first how could they be sure he was going to show up since he wasn't part of the volunteer list, and second how did they escape undetected after Peabody and Mac showed up and started CPR?"

"Easy. It was chaos at the end so anyone could have slipped out undetected. And you just noted the hall was open when you arrived, so whoever it was got in early and hid."

"What about the other clown? Where did they disappear to?"

"Did you see a third clown or was it something Josie said? The child could have been mistaken. It was a pretty chaotic evening."

Milo had a good point. "Victor said there were two and one was skinny and Kevin confirmed it right after Josie talked about the second one." I looked out the window and saw Gage jogging through the town park. In one hand was a white bag and the other a tray with drinks. What was my detective better at than bringing me a coffee and a sweet treat when I needed a zip? He paused before he crossed the street, and balancing the bag on top of the cups, he picked up what looked like a tattered piece of cloth and tossed it in the garbage bin.

I saw that Dax wasn't with him as I flung open the door and took the bag from him. I could ask about that as we walked. "Come on. We need to make a quick stop at the grange hall before we talk to a little girl about a clown."

Confusion filled his face. "What are you talking about?"

"The other clown. I think we're going to find the outfit somewhere at the grange hall and whoever was wearing it slipped out during the confusion, unnoticed in street clothes."

Chapter 11
Lily

Gage took the key to the grange hall from me. "I'll go first, just in case."

I was in a better position to protect us, but this time I'd let him do his job. After all, everyone needed their moment to be a hero or heroine and I was okay with that. "The light switch is right inside the door."

He pressed his finger to his lips and nodded that he heard me. I wanted to chuckle but remained quiet, listening to see if I could hear any unexpected noises from inside the building. Cautiously, we walked in, pausing before flicking on the lights. It seemed all clear. He reached out and flicked the switch, but nothing happened. Flicking it up and down again, the lights still didn't come on.

Tapping his arm, I whispered, "I've got this." It was a good thing Aunt Mimi taught me the spell to turning on lights. I held my hands palms up and said in a clear, but soft voice, "Lights on or lights off. The opposite of what is, is what shall be."

Instantly the room was flooded with bright light, even the dust motes in the darkest corner couldn't hide from the spectacular spell I had cast. I gave Gage a sheepish grin. "Too much?"

He laughed. "You're shining a light on the investigation, that's for sure." He took my hand and gave it a squeeze. "Life with you is never dull or ordinary." He gave me a quick kiss on the mouth and said, "Let's search the place."

Pumped with how great that spell had turned out, I said, "I could do a location spell and find it even faster."

Looking me in the eye, he said, "Speaking as a non-magical person, I'd like to do this the old-fashioned way so if I'm asked, I don't have to lie."

I pointed down an aisle. "I'm going to start near the vampire scene since that is closer to the back and work my way to the front."

Gage seemed to be hesitating.

"Unless you want to start there and I'll take the kitchen." I had serious doubts that we'd find anything useful in there since it was the family waiting area after the shooting.

"Let's stay together." He pulled a pair of latex gloves from his jacket pocket and handed them to me. "Put these on so all evidence can be preserved if we should find something."

I held out my pinkie. "I promise not to touch anything and let you handle it."

He hooked his little finger around mine and laughed. "You know I shouldn't have brought you at all, right? This is an official investigation."

I shrugged and smiled. "But you wouldn't have thought of this so soon if it wasn't for me and I could have kept the idea to myself and come on my own."

"You could have, but we know how that turns out when you go off without anyone with you."

I snapped the gloves on and gave him a side-eye. "I would have asked Nikki or even Milo to come with me."

"An extra witch would be a good idea, a familiar not so much. Unless he can do magic that I'm not aware of."

He was making way too much logical sense, so instead of continuing down this path, I pointed to the back of the hall. "Coming, Detective?"

With a saucy wink, he said, "Lead the way, Ms. Witch."

We searched every nook and hidey-hole the building had before moving into the kitchen. "I was so sure we'd find the costume. The clown must have taken it with him."

Gage was opening cabinet doors and moving the contents around to search each shelf. I joined him searching the shelves. I bent down to peer under the sink storage when a slip of bright orange caught my eye.

My breath caught. "Gage, I've found something stuffed in the hole behind the pipes!"

In a flash he was kneeling on the floor next to me and he turned on the flashlight app on his cell phone. "Can you turn your flashlight on so I can take pictures before I remove it?"

With a few taps on the screen, I held up the light and Gage took pictures from several angles before tugging on the fabric. He was careful to take his time so as not to tear it.

"Is it the costume?" I exhaled and sank back on my heels as the rest of the fabric came sliding out onto the floor in front of the sink. "How on earth did we not notice someone carrying a costume in here?"

Gage's face was grim. "We weren't in here until after Malcom's body was taken out. Peabody and Mac ushered the families in here when the EMT's took over." He shook his head. "There was plenty of time for someone to sneak in and stash the costume and before you ask, they never mentioned seeing a clown near the kitchen. They would have since they were the only two working the event. Malcom was the first unexpected clown, and the fourth is a complete mystery."

My cell phone pinged with an incoming text. I looked at it. "It's Kevin. He wants to know if we're still stopping by." Glancing at him, I stood up. "You need to stay here until you can document the new evidence."

I knew he wasn't going to like what I was about to say, but we needed to divide and conquer. "I'm going to talk to Kevin and Josie and see what I can find out. You stay here and let's meet at my place for dinner. I'll pick up a pizza and salad and we can compare notes."

He nodded. "If it's okay, I'm going to ask Peabody, Mac, and Dax to swing by so order two pizzas just in case everyone wants to eat. But I don't like this nagging feeling I have in the pit of my stomach. Our mystery person was in here with the kids. What if they heard us talking to Kevin and Josie?"

The same thought had crossed my mind and on my way to the antique store, I was going to give Aunt Mimi a call to see if I could cast a protection spell around them, and would they be safe for several days? Hopefully by that time Gage would have wrapped up the case.

"Alright, see you later." I could hear Gage talking on the phone before I got out of the kitchen door. The urgency in his voice confirmed what I felt. This was an important clue. I just didn't understand who had been the other clown, at least not yet.

. . .

Pushing open the heavy wood and glass door, I entered Bygone Antiques, the store that Kevin Valentine ran since his parents had retired. I couldn't help but smile when I saw Josie sitting behind the counter near an antique cash register. "Hi there."

Josie turned on the stool and her face lit up when she recognized me. "Hi, Lily. Daddy, look."

He gave his daughter an indulgent smile, one I had seen before when he looked at her. It was clear he adored his little girl, and the feeling was mutual.

Kevin looked in the direction of the street. "I thought Gage would be with you."

"That was the plan, but he got hung up with something and won't make it."

Josie said, "Do you want to see the painting I did in school today?" She jumped down from the stool and ran into the back room. She came back in a flash, waving a large piece of paper. Thrusting it at me, she said, "Look. I painted pumpkins like I saw at the haunted house."

I admired her artwork and gave her a smile. "Someday you might have your own art show and be famous."

She wrinkled her nose. "What does that mean?"

Kevin bent over and squeezed her shoulders in a one-armed hug. "It means Lily thinks your picture is beautiful."

Beaming, she held it out to me. "You can have it if you want."

This was a first. My heart constricted as I placed my hand over it. "Can I hang it in my bookstore?"

Josie nodded. "Sure. And when I paint a Thanksgiving picture, I can give you one of those too."

I knelt on the floor and gave her a hug. "Thank you so much. I'll hang this up when I get back to the store." I looked at Kevin as if asking him if it was okay to talk to Josie. He knew I had a few more questions about the clowns. He nodded.

"Josie, can we talk for a few minutes?"

She brushed her hair out of her eyes with the back of her hand and nodded. "Do you want to know what I learned in school today?" With a quick glance at Kevin, she said, "I tell Daddy every day when I get home."

"I'd like that, but first can we talk about the clowns from the other night?"

Kevin gestured to a couple of chairs arranged in a small seating area. "We should sit down."

Josie led the way and scooched back on an overstuffed velvet chair. "I told Daddy that the clowns need to be more polite."

I sat down close to her and waited for another minute, but she didn't say anything more. "Why is that?"

"Well, the one clown knocked the other clown on the floor and never said sorry."

"Do you remember if that was before or after the lid moved on the coffin?"

She thought for a minute and looked at Kevin who nodded for her to continue. "I thought that was funny when the lid moved, and then the mean clown pushed the other one down."

That caught my attention. What if Josie was watching the lid at the same time Malcom fell to the ground and she never mentioned it. "Josie, did you see anything else around the lid?"

Shaking her head, she said, "No. But the clown that fell down made a funny sound."

I wasn't going to push her by asking what kind. This just twisted the case in an entirely new direction. The shot hadn't come from the coffin, but one clown shot the other. The shooter was in with the families, and then they stashed the clown outfit, slipping out of the building undetected.

Kevin looked at me. "Does this help?"

I nodded. "Is there anything else you can think of, Josie?"

He glanced at his daughter. "Honey, can you run into the kitchen and get Lily a bottle of water, please."

She wriggled off the chair. "Sure, Daddy."

The moment she was on the other side of the room, he said, "Does this mean we're in danger? I had no idea there was any kind of interaction between Josie and the clowns."

"You have nothing to worry about." I couldn't tell him that Aunt Mimi helped me cast a protection spell around them since they weren't magical, but I could ease his fears. "I'm confident whoever the second clown was never realized Josie noticed any contact between them. She was a little girl enchanted with the haunted house. Nothing more than any other child in the room. Trust me, no one will hurt either of you. I give you my word."

I wasn't as confident in my skills but combined with my aunt's, they were safer than gold in Fort Knox.

"Thank you."

I thought about our conversation in the kitchen at the grange. "Kevin, you said it was Malcom who had the heart attack. Since he was wearing a costume and makeup, how did you know who it was?"

He glanced over his shoulder to where Josie had gone. "He's been a good customer since moving to Pembroke Cove and his voice is very distinctive. Josie thinks he made a funny sound when he fell, but he said, *Monni*. That's when I recognized it was him."

"From one word, you knew?"

"He had this way of drawing out his *O*'s. When he would negotiate for a purchase of something he'd say, how much *mon-ee* is this going to cost me. We used to joke about it, all in good fun."

Josie came skipping back into the room. "Daddy, I can't find the water bottles."

I stood up. "It's okay. I can get a drink in my shop." I picked up the picture she had given me. "Make sure you stop at the bookstore so you can see where I hang your painting."

She looked at Kevin. "Can we go on Saturday?"

"We can." He smiled at me. "Thank you for everything, Lily."

"You're welcome and see you soon." I waved to Josie and wandered in the direction of my store.

It was only two doors down but as I strolled, I thought about Malcom being shot by the clown. I called Gage before I went inside but checked around to make sure no one on the street could overhear my side of the conversation.

"Lily. Is everything okay?"

I didn't even have the opportunity to say hello. "I'm fine but you need to change your direction. Based on what Josie and Kevin just told me, the other clown was the person who shot Malcom."

"What are you talking about? The lid on the coffin moved and there was a hiding place in there big enough for a person."

Sometimes he was so literal it shocked me. I took a deep breath and exhaled. "What if that was just a diversion and a gun was left there on purpose. The clown shoots Malcom and somehow gets out of the costume, is escorted into the kitchen as part of a family group, was able to stick the costume under the sink in all the excitement, and then when the families are released, they leave through the front door with us never even noticing them."

He gave a low whistle. "You got all of that from a short conversation with a little girl?"

"Yes, and I'll fill you in on a few other observations she had too."

"If you're right, then this puts them potentially in danger."

Before he could hang up, I said, "Aunt Mimi and I took care of that. We've cast a protection spell around them that will last for three days. If we need to, we can cast another until you're sure they're safe."

"That's my girl, thinking on her feet and as usual one step ahead of me."

"I appreciate your appreciation of the way my brain works."

He laughed softly. "Lily, have I told you lately you really are my favorite witch?"

"Nope, but you should start to make a habit of it. I like how it sounds."

"Do me a favor and don't tell my mother." He chuckled. "But I'm sure she'd understand since she's Dad's favorite."

"Must run in the family." The wind kicked up and I zipped up my jacket. I heard my name and looked up. "I gotta go. Victor is heading in my direction and he looks upset."

Chapter 12
Gage

I looked at my phone after the line went dead. What the heck was going on and why had Lily hung up on me? The bigger question is, why was Victor going to see her? We were still processing the kitchen for clues so I couldn't leave yet. How much danger could she be in on the sidewalk in broad daylight? I took a deep calming breath, reminding myself she wasn't an ordinary shop owner. As a witch, she knew how to protect herself and if Lily needed me, she could cast a spell which she had done before, calling me to her. I refocused on the task at hand. The sooner I was done, the faster I could get to her place.

An hour later I parked my vintage truck on the street in front of Lily's house. All the lights were on and in the driveway was Steve's truck, Dax's car, and Peabody's motorcycle. What she was doing riding it on a freezing-cold night was beyond me. It was going to be an interesting evening. The door opened before I got to the front steps and Lily met me. Relief coursed through me even though I knew in my soul she was fine. She looked terrific dressed in jeans and a plum-colored cable-knit sweater. Her sable-brown eyes held a hint of laughter. I opened my arms and she ran into them. There was nothing like this feeling, holding her in my arms and for a moment I wondered if this could be every night if I followed Steve's lead.

"About time you showed up. The gang's all here." She inclined her head toward the house.

"I stopped home to pick up Brutus." As I said his name, he lumbered up the steps after sniffing every square inch of the front yard.

"Hello, sweet boy." She stroked the top of his head. Turning her eyes back to mine, she said, "Hello, sweet man," and she gave me a tender kiss. Taking my hand, she pulled me to the door and tapped her other hand against her thigh and my dog trotted after her, as if he'd follow her anywhere. I had to agree with the sentiment.

"Everyone, look who I found loitering outside."

The group greeted me with welcoming grins and Steve put a beer in my hand. He said, "I wondered if you'd get here before we polished off the pizza."

I noticed Mac was absent and there were four large pizza boxes on the countertop. "There's enough to feed half the town."

I opened my mouth to ask Lily about her conversation with Victor when she pointed at the stack of plates. "Dinner first, then we talk." She patted my arm and went to the pantry, withdrawing a couple of large bones for Brutus and Nikki's dog, Murphy, who were sprawled out in the living room.

"Are you sure Milo doesn't mind being invaded by big dogs?"

Nikki walked past me with her plate overflowing with salad and a slice of pizza hanging off the edge. "Milo and Murphy are good friends." She gave me a wink and whispered, "The familiar network is welcoming."

I glanced at Peabody, to see if she heard Nikki's statement since she wasn't part of the witch community and I didn't want to have to explain. She'd think I had gone off the deep end. "Hey, Peabody, no Mac tonight?"

"He's home with his lovely bride and beautiful baby."

I caught the wistful tone in her voice and looked at Dax, the only other single person in the room. If he made up his mind to stay in town, it would be nice to see if they would date.

"Good for him. We'll just need to bring him up to speed tomorrow."

With a brisk nod, she turned to get her dinner. Everyone was gathering in the living room and I followed suit, sitting next to Lily on the sofa. Milo stalked in, looked at everyone, and then meowed at Lily.

She patted the arm of the sofa and he slunked out of the living room. I wished I understood familiar. I chuckled and she looked at me with her eyebrow arched.

"What's so funny?"

"I was just thinking it would be nice if I was like Dr. Doolittle and could understand what Milo is saying when he meows."

She picked up her pizza and frowned. "You don't want to know."

I wondered what had gone on between the two of them. Maybe he wasn't happy about the dogs invading his space, but Lily and Nikki had said Milo was good with them. Could he have been talking about the case? Did he even get involved in these kinds of things? I made a mental note to talk to Lily about how this familiar and witch thing worked between the two of them.

She nudged my leg with hers. "Why are you on edge tonight?"

"What?"

"You're doing that thing when you wrinkle your forehead and have a faraway look in your eye. Is it the case?"

"Partly but like you said, we'll talk about that later."

Her brow quirked again.

But I didn't elaborate on what was preying on my mind. Taking a bite of the pizza, I said, "Meat lovers, my favorite."

An hour later, everyone was stuffed from dinner and Lily had dragged her clue board into the living room. She was standing next to it and waited for everyone's attention to focus on her.

"I've uncovered some important clues in the last few hours." She drew a line under the columns *Suspect* and *Motive*. Then she added skinny next to the word clown. "Today I talked with Josie Valentine who told me that when she was watching the lid on the coffin move, the skinny clown bumped into Malcom and knocked him to the ground and didn't apologize." She let that sink in for a moment. "Does everyone see what I'm getting at?"

Nikki said, "The clown didn't have any manners?"

Dax inched to the edge of his chair. "The shot didn't come from the coffin. Malcom was shot at close range by our mystery clown."

"Now why the autopsy didn't indicate that is beyond me." She gave Dax a pointed look and then turned her attention to Gage. "That's right and Gage, I'm not sure if you caught this, but when we talked to Kevin after the shooting, he used Malcom's name when no one else knew who he was. When I asked him about it today, he said that Malcom had been a frequent customer at the antique store and as he was falling to the ground, he said a word that sounded like money."

Peabody was nodding, her face serious. "Taking a leap, could that suggest Malcom was trying to indicate it had something to do with the fraud case?"

Dax chimed in, "But is it? We know from the information we found at his house he was writing an investigative piece on real estate fraud. What if he had been asked to meet someone at the haunted house to gather evidence? People are dressed in costumes so an informant could remain anonymous."

I was impressed with Lily; she had a simple conversation with Josie and she was able to glean an important clue. "This is solid information, Lily, but it doesn't bring us any closer to knowing who the other clown was."

"Not yet, but can't you test the costume for DNA? And what about gunpowder residue?"

Dax said, "We can have both those tests run but it might not be quick. This isn't a one-hour television show. It can take time and if the DNA doesn't match anything in our system, it won't get us any closer to discovering their identity."

I asked, "What about Victor coming to see you at the end of the day?"

She tapped the chalk to her lip. "That was odd. He flagged me down on the sidewalk and he was so jittery. I think he was fishing to see if I knew more than I had let on when we talked to him this morning. He was looking for a book on the history of the town for his mother. Which, of course, I sold to him."

Peabody was studying the chalkboard. "So, what I don't understand, if the shooter wasn't inside the coffin, why modify it? Or could it have been the original plan and for some reason it was changed at the last minute?"

She had a point. I said, "Maybe there were too many people to be able to sneak in and out. The shooter had to have known it would be crazy once people went to assist Malcom."

Lily said, "We need to go under the assumption that Malcom was planning on meeting someone. Maybe they had promised information on the article he was writing. It can't be something else since Dax's fraud case is the only ongoing issue in town."

She gave me a look as if I should confirm. Without hesitation, I said, "Correct."

"Has anyone been able to access the files on his laptop?" Lily looked at me and then Dax.

"Mac was working on that earlier, well, before we got called to the grange hall," Peabody said. "But he'll be back at it in the morning."

Steve set his plate on the side table, "I'm not Sherlock Holmes but what about phone records? Don't the police usually check out the call log?"

With a nod, I said, "We could but his phone hasn't been recovered. It wasn't in his car, at his house, or even on him."

Lily wrote down *Phone?* under his name. "We're missing too many pieces of the puzzle to get much further tonight." She then wrote *Clown 2* next to *Shooter* and continued to tap the chalk on her jeans. "What about

Victor? He said he went behind the curtain to get more candy. Was that before or after Malcom slumped to the floor? Could he have shot the gun and then tossed it aside using the moving lid as a distraction?"

"Unlikely. The gun we found didn't kill him," I said. "Besides, all the witnesses said he was holding the candy bowl and from where he was standing, he wouldn't have had a clear shot and the coroner confirmed Malcom was shot in the back." I hoped Lily didn't catch what I had just said and drill me about the gun.

Lily shook her head. "With all the confusion, people could think they remembered the events in a certain way. No. At this point, Victor is definitely involved. I just don't know how."

Nikki stood and held out her hand to Steve. "Help me clean up the kitchen and we can take off." She gave Lily a quick wink and I had to wonder what the ladies were up to now.

Peabody and Dax followed them into the kitchen. I got up and crossed the room to Lily. "I can tell by that look in your eye there is more bubbling beneath the surface."

She slipped her arms around my neck. "You mean like a cauldron bubbling. I don't have one of those." Taking a step back, she snapped her fingers, "Wait a minute. There was a Teddy Roberts pen on Malcom's desk." She smacked the palm of her hand to her head. "Why didn't I think of that before now? Have you discovered any more pens that could be connected to the crime?"

"Yeah. Mac found one near the coffin. He thinks it must have been used to prop up one corner to make it easier for our suspect to lift it up and enter, then exit the bottom of the coffin."

Her eyes gleamed. "It's another thread tying this back to Dax's case. We have to tell him before he leaves."

"He already knows."

"Not about Malcom's house." She slipped from my arms and hurried into the kitchen. Milo was sitting in the doorway and loudly meowed at me before following Lily. I got the feeling he'd just given me a sharp reprimand.

Lily had Dax cornered. "Two Teddy Roberts Real Estate pens have been found so far. It's an important clue."

He glanced in my direction before looking at her again. "You're right, this case is connected to mine. But it has many layers. I need to get the person at the top. This shooter was more than likely a hired gun trying to quash the article. I can continue to take out the small fish, but I need the great white shark to stop this, not just in Pembroke Cove but in other areas too. In addition, we need to solve Malcom's murder. He deserves justice and his final article to be released. I need to stay focused on the larger objective and that is to get to the top of the food chain." He glanced in my direction again. "Lily, you need to promise me that if you find anything that indicates who this person is, you'll tell me. Do not go off on your own. With what happened to Malcom, it shows they'll do anything to bury their secrets."

I commended Dax for sharing. "He's right, Lily. We're not looking at a jilted girlfriend or a coworker this time. This is serious business."

She popped her hands on her hips. "It's always serious and I don't take any of this lightly. But this was at an event I was coordinating; children could have been harmed. Heck, I still don't know if it will register with Josie Valentine at some point what really happened right next to her. I pray it doesn't and we need to send a message to this person that he chose to tangle with the wrong witch."

I reached out to her, and she took a step back. Did she realize she just referred to herself as a witch? Did Peabody and Dax catch it?

Dax's voice morphed into his slow, soft drawl, but his eyes were intense and solely focused on Lily. "No one wants to get this person more than me and not because of the fraud case but Malcom was doing the right thing. His article would have brought them to justice and for that I promise you, I will find the persons responsible and they will be held accountable for all their crimes."

Was it my imagination or did Lily begin to relax the moment Dax started to talk to her?

She looked from Dax, to Peabody, and then finally to me, chin thrust upward. "Don't ask me to step aside. I promise I'll be mindful of who and what is at play here, but I need to do what I can to help." She dipped her chin and leveled her gaze at me. "And I won't go off on my own investigation. Promise."

Dax's face relaxed and my insides did the same. One thing about Lily was she never went back on her word.

She took my hand and looked at Peabody. "Gage, Sharon, do you think we'll be able to open the haunted house up again by Saturday? After all, I dangled it to Victor and I'd like to get our spook on again. We need to finish raising money for our upcoming holiday events."

I wanted to say yes but I wasn't sure, considering we had overlooked the clown costume. Peabody said, "What if we find a new location for the haunted house? I bet we could get volunteers to move everything."

Lily's face grew pensive. "We've always held it at the grange, and I can't think of another place that would work."

"What about Marshall Stone's farm? He had the corn maze and I know he hasn't mowed it down yet. Obviously, it would be outside, but when I talked to him earlier today, he was happy to agree and I checked the weather forecast. It's going to be clear, but cold."

Lily looked around at her friends gathered in her kitchen. With a wide grin, she said, "Sharon, that is a great idea. Now who's up for a little work?"

Chapter 13
Lily

I placed a checkmark next to Corbin Marks' name on my list. He was quick to volunteer to move scenes out to Marshall's place. Sharon Peabody was fast becoming one of my favorite people, to find a solution to our situation was above and beyond. Next, I needed to talk to Gretchen Wilson to see if she could spare a few hours. She answered on the third ring.

"Gretchen Wilson Realty, this is Gretchen."

She sounded perky. "Hi, it's Lily Michaels. I hope I didn't catch you at a bad time."

"Not at all, Lily. How can I help you today? Are you interested in selling or buying?"

Always the salesperson. "No. I'm happy in my cottage but if anything changes, you'll be the first person I call."

"Well then, how can I help?"

"We've decided to reopen the haunted house and we're rebuilding everything at Marshall Stone's farm. He has graciously allowed us to set up the scenes near the corn maze and as luck would have it, the weather will be clear this weekend."

"That's great news."

Still sounding upbeat was a good sign in my book. "I was hoping we could count on you to recreate some of the sets. We can't take anything from the grange hall since it is still the scene of, well, you know. This will be on a smaller scale, but we have a ton of volunteers and Corbin Marks is willing to help and Tucker's Hardware Store is going to donate supplies."

"That sounds like a lot of work, but I think I can clear my schedule. Real estate sales slow as it gets closer to the holiday season. What time do you need me?"

"Can you make it today at noon at the farm?" I placed another checkmark on my paper with a happy face next to it.

"I have to make one stop and then I'll be along."

"Perfect. We're going to do our best to create ten scenes and have the hay bales and cornstalks create paths through the area. I'll see you later."

"Lily? Before you go, I was wondering if I could ask your advice?"

"Since you're helping me, I'm happy to return the favor. What's up?"

"Well, the strangest thing happened early this morning. I got a phone call and I couldn't tell if it was a male or female, but they asked me if I wanted to take over for Teddy Roberts."

I leaned forward in my chair as if I could hear more clearly. "Help someone find a home to buy?"

"At first that's what I thought they were talking about. You know since Teddy passed, I'm the only licensed agent in town so naturally business is falling in my direction."

Good thing it was her slow season, but I sounded more

like Milo being snarky than me. "They weren't looking to buy a home?"

"No, they said they were looking for a new partner and would I be interested. They went into a bit more detail and I declined and got off the phone as quickly as possible. Do you think I should report it to Gage or that man, Dax Peters? The rumor mill is active, saying he is the guy running that investigation. I mean, maybe I'm blowing this all out of proportion, but it seemed odd."

My heartbeat quickened. This was a solid lead, but I didn't want to scare her, so I said, "Dax is leading the investigation that is connected with Teddy's improper sales tactics and he's been working out of the police station. I would suggest you stop at the station and tell Dax and Gage at the same time. This way they can ask you any additional questions and you won't have to repeat yourself."

An audible exhale reached my ears. "I knew you'd have the best answer. Thank you, Lily, and I'll see you at noon."

I twirled in my kitchen chair and looked at my clue board. This needed to be added as a new wrinkle. But why had it taken so long for whoever was behind the real estate scheme to reach out? Teddy died six weeks ago.

"Milo?" I called down the hall. Without a response, I called out again, "I'm fixing tuna, do you want some?"

Seconds later I heard a thump on the floor and the sound of four little paws carrying him to the kitchen.

"Did you say tuna?" He saw I was sitting down and not opening a can of anything. "Are you trying to trick me?"

He started to turn when I said, "Wait. I'll get the treat, but I need to bounce a few things off you."

He jumped to the chair and then to the table. "I wondered when you'd finally get around to discussing this case with me."

I gave him a side-eye. "Have you been holding out on me?"

He gave me his version of a kitty eye roll. "Have you bothered to ask?"

He had me on that one. "I'm sorry. One of these days I'll realize I have the best ally possible right under my roof." I got up and withdrew a can of tuna from the cabinet, popped the top, and put some in a bowl along with the juice and placed it on the table. "Peace offering?"

With a swish of his tail and a quick headbutt to my arm, he said, "I forgive you, my dear witch." He nibbled on the tuna and I waited until he had finished which gave me time to formulate my questions and thoughts.

"When you've been out making your rounds with your friends, have you heard anything about Malcom Sloane?"

"Like what, if he was magical and had a familiar?"

"No. When I was at his house, I didn't see any signs of a cat or dog. I meant, has anyone ever noticed who he might spend time with, if he was a solitary person or had friends. That kind of thing."

"I can ask around but I've never heard a peep about the man. It's like he was an average guy living a dull life."

Leave it to Milo to think a non-magical person's life was dull. He must not think much of my old life prior to discovering I was a witch a few short months ago. "I'd appreciate if you could see what you can find out. He had to have been meeting with someone in town since he went to the event dressed up for a specific purpose and wandered around during the family hour."

In his low kitty growl, he said, "It's a shame, all those kids." He swished his tail. "I'll see what I can discover. Do you need anything else?"

I could feel that this murder got under his fur. "You

were at the hall that night. You didn't see or hear anything out of the ordinary?"

"I don't know anything for sure, but I think the gun near the coffin was fake. You need to ask Gage about it, or has he already confirmed it was the weapon used to shoot Malcom?"

As I sat there, I realized he said the gun wasn't the murder weapon but nothing more. I gave Milo a sharp look. "Why do you think it was fake?"

"If your retelling of the events is correct and one clown shot the other, then there would not have been an opportunity to drop the same gun next to the coffin. Any person with half a brain would not leave a loaded gun around kids."

The thought of a child picking up a loaded gun caused my blood to freeze. I had to ask Gage if it was a fake. Even if he wouldn't tell me much else, I needed to have that ease my mind and if he played his tap dance game, I'd demand to know. Especially since we were getting ready to hold the haunted house again.

"Ms. Witch, your detective had best watch out if that fierce look on your face is any judge of the thoughts going through your head right now."

"Why wouldn't Gage tell me about that gun? I can't believe I overlooked an obvious clue. Am I losing my touch?" I jumped up and began to pace the width of my kitchen. What else had I missed? Nope. I stood by my clue board. It was a solid path to solving this, but I think my biggest challenge was working in close contact with Gage. He made me err on the side of process; I was a doer. Following my instincts hadn't steered me wrong—well, except when I confronted Teddy's killer. That was a tad reckless but I was able to save myself and it all had turned out fine. I was still here to tell the tale. "You know what, Milo?"

"I'm not sure I want to know what just popped into your head. But go on, I won't be able to stop the roll you're on."

"I don't need Gage or anyone else's permission to follow the clues where they might lead me. I promised that I wouldn't go off alone and deliberately put myself in danger, but I'm not going to be the good little witch and stand by while some gun-toting nutjob could saunter into our next haunted house looking to scare our townspeople. Who knows for sure, maybe enough damage has been done to keep people away. But I'm keeping my eyes peeled, I"ll encourage our volunteers to work hard, and we are going to have a great event."

Milo stood on the table and stretched in my direction. I scooped him up. "I have a plan. Now you need to get out there and see what you can find for information and just for the extra help, we'll have something extra tasty for dinner tonight."

He rubbed his head against my chin and growled affectionately. "I vote for chicken livers."

"And I veto." I kissed his head and set him down. "Nice try."

When I finally arrived at the corn maze, Marshall was overseeing the volunteers. I gave him a wave and hurried to where Nikki was setting up a refreshment area with drinks and cookies.

"Hey, girl," she said, "I was beginning to think you got lost."

"Sorry, I was talking with Milo and looking over my clue board again and for the life of me I can't figure out who's the skinny clown. Motive I get, trying to stop the reporter from spilling all the details sure, but why did they choose to meet at the vampire scene, and do we need to take precautions that something like this doesn't happen again on Saturday?"

She handed me an oversized molasses cookie with a sprinkling of orange-colored sugar on the top. I broke it in half, eating a bite without even tasting it.

"Lily, if the motive behind what happened with Malcom was to stop his article, then it's over. We don't know for sure who he was going to submit the article to, right?"

I shook my head. "Dax thinks it was going to be published in *The Post* but who knows for sure. And you're right, there is no article without Malcom. I guess I'm freaking out over nothing. This event will go off without a hitch as long as we can get people to come."

Nikki smiled at someone over my shoulder, and I looked. "Aunt Mimi, what are you doing out here?"

"I came to offer my help and Nate told Corbin he'd pitch in and build a few things that couldn't be moved." She patted my cheek. "Don't worry, this time, there will be no secret hiding places allowed."

"Do you think people will come?" I ate more of the cookie and offered the other half to my aunt who graciously declined but took a chocolate chip cookie from the tray.

"Before we drove out of town, I stopped at Bee Bee's Boutique and Twisted Scissors; you and I know how easy it is to get information going from both of these stores. I'm sure by the end of the day, people will be eager to come and donate to support the next good cause."

Throwing my arms around her neck, I hugged her tight. "Thank you, Aunt Mimi. I should have called you instead of worrying about it all morning."

"I'm here now and have that part under control. Is there anything else I can do?"

I looked from my aunt's perfectly shined black leather boots, to pressed jeans, cashmere sweater, and leather jacket. There was no way she was prepared to build scenes or anything else in the freezing cold.

"I was going to reopen the bookstore after my lunch break, but would you like to cover the store for me this afternoon and I can stay here?"

"That I can do." With a quick kiss on my cheek, she reminded me to stay warm and whispered there was a down jacket in my car. Which meant somehow the woman had conjured up warm clothing for me to wear. She went to say goodbye to Nate, and I headed in the direction of my car. Time to get busy.

I rubbed my hands together and pulled out my checklist. First up was the fortune teller table for Dax. Corbin was walking by with two-by-four boards balanced on his shoulder and a tool pouch slung low on his hips. I couldn't help but notice he was as skinny as the boards he carried.

"Hey, Lily, this is going to be a fun time," he said. "The reason why we're out here stinks, of course, but it will add to the ambience on Saturday night."

"I agree." I fell in step next to him. "Any idea what we plan to do for the fortune teller scene?"

He nodded in Marshall's direction. "He was gonna scare up a small wood table with a couple of benches. I think he said it was his picnic table, but not the kind you see at the park but a round version."

"Okay, good. I'll check in with Marshall. Also, Nikki's laid out snacks; make sure you get some. This cold air will sap your strength."

He gave me a salute. "See you later." He headed deeper into the corn maze, and I should have asked him which scene he was working on but that didn't matter. I could track him down later. Instead, I jogged to catch up to Marshall.

And my steps slowed as Gage headed in my direction and by the look on his face, the news wasn't good. He gestured for me to follow him away from any people.

When we got closer to the cars, he said, "I have some news."

I crossed my arms over my chest and narrowed my eyes. "Let me guess, the gun at the scene of the crime was never shot because it was a fake?"

His eyes widened briefly and he didn't need to confirm it. The dip in his chin said it all. "That's true, but not what I was going to tell you."

"Then what?"

"The skinny clown is a woman. There was makeup on the collar."

I shook my head. "Gage, what are you thinking? Clowns wear makeup..."

Chapter 14
Lily

Later that afternoon I was in my bookstore and Aunt Mimi had gone home. I loved this time of day when it was before the last-minute rush of customers on their way home and it was typically just me, Milo, and the books.

I decided to brew a cup of tea before I dove into my book order. I was a little behind for holiday shopping, but I was confident I'd get what I needed in plenty of time. Walking into the back room, I discovered Milo was stretched out in front of the door, a sliver of sunshine bathing my gray tabby in a golden glow.

Bending over, I ran my fingers down the length of his body. He lazily opened one eye and blinked. "Why are you interrupting my catnap?"

"I'm making tea and thought a little catnip was in order for you."

He stretched his upper body into a half-upright pose. "I like that idea." He got to all four paws and stretched like a downward dog yoga position. "How were things at the farm?"

After adding water to the teakettle, I leaned against the counter. I was more confident now than I had been at the farm. "It's going well. Everyone is working together and I left Corbin in charge of the volunteers since he's our resident expert when it comes to woodworking. Nikki is helping things along with treats and a little magic from time to time. And Nate, as usual, is like glue holding all the parts together and understands we're trying to create each scene like it's a standalone for maximum scare output."

Milo hopped to a wooden chair. "What does that mean? You're putting a lot of space between each area?"

"Yes, it was Corbin's idea and not something we could have done at the grange hall. There wasn't enough space. The walkways will be lit just enough for people to move safely from one area to the other with a lot of spookiness built in. It's genius."

It was good to keep busy as I gave Milo the rundown. It also helped to clear my head. What was Gage thinking by jumping to the conclusion the skinny clown was a woman just because there was makeup on the collar? And later we would revisit the fact that he never mentioned it was a decoy gun. I filled the tea infuser with some of my mom's special relaxation blend and placed it in the pot. My honey jar was empty in the cabinet, but I had a small display out front.

"Why the frowny face?" he asked.

Shaking my head, I was about to tell him when I heard the bell above the front door jingle. I poured the water into the teapot and went out front.

"Vonni, this is a pleasant surprise." I quickly put a welcoming smile on my face. She was the last person I expected to see since Victor had been here last night buying a book for her.

As with the first time we met, she was impeccably dressed in an elegant pantsuit which was perfect for a business meeting in the city but not a blustery day in Pembroke Cove. Her hair was in loose waves framing her angular features and her makeup was model perfect. She looked as if she were about to hit the runway, not the sidewalk.

The same polite smile was on her face, but her eyes were still cold. "Victor was in yesterday and picked up a book for me on the local history which I'm enjoying very much. But I was hoping you could help me pick up a couple of novels, maybe romantic suspense. I just love a good mystery, don't you?"

"Are you interested in historical mysteries or contemporary? I have a good mix." I walked to one of the aisles. "You can take a look here and see if something piques your interest. If not, I'll pull a couple that might."

Vonni followed me and looked around. "The store is very quiet. Is your business always like this?"

Taken aback by her direct approach regarding my store, I said, "This is normal for this time of day. Like most shops that surround the square, we're busy earlier and later."

"Good for you."

That statement made me feel as if she was trying to lift my spirits and why, I wasn't sure. "Take your time browsing."

Her stare followed me as I went into the back room, annoyed I had forgotten to grab the honey while I'd been out front. I really needed my relaxation tea now as this woman was borderline annoying. Milo hopped down and wandered into the shop. I was sure my familiar was going to find a new place to snooze.

I filled my mug with fragrant tea, and skipping the honey, I went back to my counter. Vonni was still in the mystery aisle and I sipped my tea. When she finally approached the cash register, she had three books and handed them to me.

"This morning my son was telling me the police still don't have any real leads on who killed that poor man right in front of Victor's Halloween scene last weekend. I was wondering if your friend, Gage is it, mentioned anything to you. I'm not sure I feel safe walking around town alone."

This was why Vonni had come into the shop; she was fishing for information. "They're getting closer to discovering the truth. Our police department is very good."

She pursed her lips and withdrew her wallet. "I heard something about a special investigator from DC. Is that true, they had to bring in outside help?" She handed me her credit card as I rang up her purchases and she added some note cards, a pen, and a small bag of mints to her pile.

"Dax has been here for several months. He's working on a case that I'm not at liberty to talk about."

"Victor has met him a few times and mentioned he's a Southerner."

I glanced at her, my eyebrow spiking into an arch. What was she getting at, that being south of Boston was somehow bad?

"He's very good at his job."

Nodding, she said, "That is a relief. I would hate to think Victor had chosen to relocate to a crime-ridden town."

I handed her back her credit card and slipped her purchases into a canvas tote bag.

"Oh, Lily, I didn't buy the bag."

"It's free with all purchases over a certain amount." I gave her my best shopkeeper smile. "And your order qualified."

"You really shouldn't give away your profits like that."

She took the bag, "But it is a lovely touch. Thank you very much and"—she looked around—"I just love your little shop. I'm sure I'll be back soon."

"My hours are listed on the front window." I waited until the door was firmly closed and she was crossing the street, heading in the direction of The Sweet Spot before I shook off the mood she had cast. I had to chuckle. If she was looking for gossip, Tucker's Hardware was the better choice.

The soft thud of a kitty pounce drew my attention away from Vonni. In his usual low kitty growl, he said, "What did you think of your customer?"

"She doesn't think much of our charming town or its residents and less of my business methods. But the joke's on her if she thinks trolling for information will get her anywhere." I pointed to her entering William's bakery. "For a reason I can't fathom, she's very interested in what has happened."

"Maybe Victor asked her to come down and scope things out. The man had someone shot right in front of his eyes. That had to be unnerving."

Was it possible that Victor hired someone to shoot Malcom? After all, he might be trying to acquire property in town and not for anything other than to get good deals. Maybe he wanted to buy single homes and flip them for a lot of money as vacation properties. It was a little out of his scope, but anything was possible. I crossed to the window and waited until Vonni came out of the bakery. The scowl on her face, which was easy to see from where I stood, brought a smile to mine.

"Ms. Witch?" Milo hopped to the window seat and looked in the direction I was staring. "What are you thinking about?"

"I need to go back to the grange hall and walk through where everyone was again. Maybe Victor went into the back not to get more candy but to get a gun since as far as I know the weapon used to shoot Malcom has not been located."

"Want some company?"

I started to say I'd meet him at home, but I promised Gage I would be careful and taking Milo was always a good idea. He had helped me escape the library when I had been poking around while following the clues for Flora Gray's death. "Yes, we'll leave when I close the store and you can be the lookout."

"Then I'm going to squeeze in a short nap before we go." Milo jumped down from the window seat and trotted down an aisle. I suspected he was headed to the cozy corner I had set up for him at the end of the mystery section. Before he disappeared completely, he said, "Go read your book; you've got time to practice a new spell."

Calling after him, I asked, "What are you talking about?" But, of course, just like always, he didn't answer me. I stamped my foot in frustration and muttering to myself, I said, "I'll open the book but it never shows me what I think I need."

I grabbed a jar of honey on my way past the display. At least I could perk up my tea while I was studying.

At five on the dot, I closed my big book of *Practical Beginnings*, locked the register, and called to Milo. "Time to head out. Are you coming?"

He trotted around the corner and hopped onto the counter. "You can't leave without me, but first tell me. What did you learn?"

"There was a spell on how to open a locked door and the self-protection spell popped up again."

He nodded. "Both useful for different reasons. Did you work on both?"

"I memorized the locked door spell, but I focused on perfecting the protection spell since that will be more useful in the short term."

"Are we walking to the hall?"

It wasn't far, just behind the town hall at the opposite end of the square, but the wind had kicked up and it would be easier to hop in the car and drive home after I was done looking for clues. "No, it's wicked cold and no sense drawing attention to us as we enter the building."

"People will see us no matter what." Milo hopped down and headed to the back door.

"Not if we slip in the back entrance. I can park in the lot near the kitchen and there is only one small light so we should be able to go in virtually undetected."

He stopped and waited for me to slip on my coat even though he could have gone out his little kitty door. "Have you ever gone anywhere in this town when people haven't noticed you?"

"I'm not sure if I should take that as a compliment or an insult?" I adjusted the collar on my bright-green wool coat and groaned. "This isn't the best option for blending in."

"Maybe you should call Gage and ask him to let you inside instead of sneaking around."

Flashing Milo a frosty look, I opened the door. "I'm sure this idea is off the mark, so why point out that I've lost my touch."

Milo didn't walk out the door and I scooped him up as he asked, "Who said that?"

"Why haven't I figured this case out yet? We have one

dead clown, one skinny clown, and a suspicious vampire who's into real estate. I don't want Gage to think I couldn't see the obvious answer that has been right in front of me."

Milo growled, "If it was obvious, Detective Cutie would already have Victor Seidel under arrest. As far as I can tell, you're the only person thinking outside the box."

I closed and locked the shop door as I held him close. "Then let's go solve a murder."

Chapter 15
Gage

As I was driving back to the police station, I noticed there was a light flickering inside the grange hall. I stopped my police sedan next to the curb and scanned the area for any cars. But other than a few vehicles in the town hall parking lot, all was quiet. I waited to see if the light would appear again, but it hadn't. Must have been a trick of the streetlight. Besides, I added a new lock to the hall so any keys floating around wouldn't unlock it. Satisfied nothing was happening, I eased back onto the road.

I hadn't seen Lily in almost twenty-four hours which was understandable since we both had so much going on, me with the investigation and her with getting the haunted house relocated and ready for opening in two days. I wanted to help but Dax was getting pressure to wrap his case up and we both agreed, we were close to finding out who was running the operation.

My cell pinged and I answered. "Detective Erikson."

"Hi, this is Gretchen Wilson and I was wondering if I could come by the station tonight. Something odd happened and Lily thought I should tell you and Dax Peters at the same time."

This was interesting and if Lily suggested Gretchen talk to me that meant she was one step ahead of me, again. "I'm on my way there now. Can you meet me be there in fifteen minutes?"

"Thank you, I'll see you soon."

When I disconnected from the call with Gretchen, I dialed Dax.

"Peters here."

"Are you at the station?"

"Yes, I was just leaving." His answer was laced with curiosity.

"Wait for me. I just got a call from Gretchen Wilson and she asked to talk to us but didn't say what it was about."

"When?"

"I'm on my way and I'll be there in five minutes and she'll be about ten minutes behind me. First, I want to run a couple of things by you."

Dax paused. "I'll be here and I got a report back you will want to see."

With a flick of my blinker, I turned on to Doenut Drive and the police station loomed directly ahead. Lights blazed from every window and even as a child I felt that this was the only place I wanted to work.

I entered through the back door. Some of the administrative staff offices were dark, but the desk officer lifted a hand when he saw me.

I called, "Hey, Lou. When Gretchen Wilson gets here, give me a call."

"You got it, Detective."

Down the hall, Dax was sitting in the office next to

mine. A paper cup with what looked like cold coffee sat on the desk. He looked up. "Tough day?"

"I was back at the Sloane house trying to see if we overlooked anything. I can't figure out how the person got in, not Lily but the suspect for his murder."

"She said the glass door was unlocked. Maybe Mr. Sloane didn't lock his doors; he thought living in a small town meant nothing bad ever happened here."

"I found a sheet of plywood in his garage and it was intact, so that loose end is tied up." I slumped into the empty chair next to the desk. "That's what I think too, but it doesn't give me anything to go on. Whoever was there knows Lily was poking around too."

Dax held up his hand. "I get it. You think there's a target on her back now. I've come to the same conclusion."

He slid a couple of pages across the desk. "Bad news and more bad news."

I gave him a quick look before skimming the papers. "The bullets that killed Malcom Sloane are from a generic 9mm and we have no way to trace them back to the shooter without the gun." I placed the papers on the desk. "Got any good news?"

"An unsolved case about five years ago in Chicago had the same shell casing left behind. We know that the gun was used at least twice but there is nothing else that ties the two cases together."

"What was that case?"

"Attempted house robbery but the people were home, and while the perp was escaping, he shot once and the bullet lodged in the upper clapboard of the house. Obviously, it wasn't intended to hit anyone, just give the perp time to get away."

"That's lucky. I take it the person was never caught?"

He shook his head. "Another cold case."

Lou came around the corner and stuck his head in the office. "Detective, Ms. Wilson is here. I had her wait in the conference room near the lobby."

"Thanks, we'll be right there." I got up, "For the record, she's already talked to Lily."

Dax's grin spread over his face. "Why doesn't that surprise me?"

Gretchen was twisting her handbag strap around her hand when we walked in. She looked like a cornered rabbit in Mr. MacGregor's garden. I extended my hand, but she didn't take it. "Can I get you a coffee or water?"

She shook her head. "No." Looking at Dax, she said, "Are you the special investigator from DC?"

He pulled out a chair and sat down across from her. In a warm, friendly tone that was laced with a bit of Southern charm, he said, "Yes. Dax Peters. It's nice to meet you, Ms. Wilson."

A weak smile appeared on her lips and she glanced away. "Thank you for agreeing to meet with me. I was talking to Lily this morning about helping out with the redo of the haunted house and all, which is a pleasant surprise that Marshall Stone agreed to let us have it at his place, and that the weather is going to be fair."

I hoped she'd take a breath after that long run-on sentence. But like most people who had nothing to worry about by talking to the police, they were the ones who were the most nervous. "Marshall is a good man."

"Well, like I said, I was talking to Lily, and I mentioned a strange phone call I received at the office. Ever since Teddy Roberts died, my real estate business has been busy since he was my only competition. Anyway, I got this call and a person asked me if I want to take over working with them, like Teddy Roberts. At first, I thought they were talking about helping them buy a home or maybe a commercial property. Before I could ask what they would be interested in looking at, they said it was the special arrangement they had with him and it would be worth a lot of money to me if I helped them."

Dax never moved even as I leaned in closer. "And what did you say?"

"I thanked them for calling, but that I couldn't help them. Teddy and I did not conduct business in the same manner."

Tapping a pen on the tabletop, Dax asked, "Male or female caller?"

"That's the odd thing. I couldn't tell. Their voice was kind of funny sounding, like it was muffled or something."

I glanced at Dax. "Any background noise of any kind?"

"Not that I could tell. It was really quiet and my office is always quiet. It helps me focus on my work."

"Did this person say anything else?" Dax's tone had deepened, an indication to me he was laser-focused.

Gretchen looked from Dax to me, the worry evident as her forehead creased. "Gage, did I do the wrong thing?"

"No. Not engaging was the right thing to do and coming to us was good too."

She let go of a ragged breath. "I was worried. After talking to Lily, I half expected the person to call again."

Curious, I said, "Did Lily suggest they might?"

"Oh no, not at all. But bad people don't take no for an answer, at least they don't in the movies and on television."

Dax said, "Gretchen," his voice loaded once again with that comforting Southern drawl. He used it a few times over the last few months when questioning people and it always seemed to help whoever he was talking to. "The good news, and I'm being honest, in my experience bad people like to prey on others who are weak. By you taking control of the situation right up front and saying no, that put you in control. It doesn't sound like you were indecisive; you declined and did it with professionalism. I think you handled it just right and telling us helps us help you."

"Detective Peters, thank you. That makes me feel better." She pushed back her chair and the metal legs scraped across the tile floor as she stood up. "If they call back, I'll let you know right away." She held out her hand to me.

I stood and shook it. "Do me a favor, and tell us before you tell Lily."

She nodded, her cheeks growing pink. "I'm sorry but I didn't know what to do and since you and Lily are close, I just thought I'd get her opinion."

"It's fine. But Detective Peters and I would like to make sure that all information is confidential until we're certain it poses no harm to anyone."

She nodded again and I thought her head might get tired from bobbing up and down. "I was so nervous to come here. It took hours for me to build up the courage to even call you."

Dax took her hand in his and held it for a moment. "Never be afraid to talk to us. We're here to help."

A flush rose in her cheeks again, but this time I was certain it wasn't from embarrassment but the soothing tone in Dax's voice. "Thank you again. And remember, if you need any help in real estate, I'm your girl."

He seemed to be at a loss for words with the double entendre, so I bridged the awkward gap. "Thank you, Gretchen. Be careful driving home and I appreciate you helping Lily out with the event too."

"Anytime, Gage." She looked at Dax and smiled, "Goodbye, Detective Peters."

"Good night, Ms. Wilson."

I watched as she made her way through the lobby and out the front door. "Dax, I think you have a new fan."

"Ms. Wilson seems like a good person, coming in and letting us know she was approached by whoever and that they're looking for a new partner."

I clapped him on the shoulder. "That's not what I'm talking about and you know it."

He shook his head. "If we crack this case, I'll be headed back to the city, leaving small-town life to you, Lily, and the others."

"Let me ask you a question." I perched on the edge of the conference table.

His eyes narrowed as he asked, "Which is what?"

"How many friends do you have, outside of Pembroke Cove?"

He shifted his weight from one foot to the other. "I work with a team of people and we hang out sometimes. Why do you ask?"

I held up my hand. "Nope, I'm not done with my questions before you can ask some of your own."

He pulled out a chair and sat down. "If I'm going to be interrogated, I should get more comfortable. I've seen you talk to suspects before and you do this whole waiting game thing to get people to spill their guts."

I grinned. "And it always works. But seriously, you've made friends here. Nikki and Steve, me and Lily, and I'm sure there are others. You've carved out a spot here. Have you ever thought of changing your life and starting over?"

"Here? I've never been a small-town kind of a guy. I like being able to get Chinese takeout at two in the morning."

With a laugh, I said, "How often do you need takeout when the rest of the world is sleeping?"

He grinned. "Never, but it's an option."

"I'm gonna butt in here."

He grinned. "Like you haven't already?"

His relaxed posture told me I could push a little more. "You've started to find your groove here. Give it some thought about hanging around after we wrap up the case." I stood. "Now I need to call my girl and see if there's a chance we can have dinner tonight. Who knows with the way her mind works; she might have even solved our case for us."

Dax got up. "If she has, give me a shout. Then all we need to do is make an arrest and fill out the paperwork."

"Consider it done." I heard my phone ping. "I'll bet that's her now."

"Have a good night, Gage, and I'll give some thought to what you said."

"That's all I ask, my friend." I glanced at the screen. "Hold on. Lily texted she wants to know if we can meet her at home and to bring dinner. She has a few things to share about the case."

Dax hovered in the doorway. "I won't be a third wheel?"

"Lily specifically included you in the text." I held out my phone. "See for yourself."

He grinned. "Then where do we get dinner from?"

I didn't have to think twice. "The Clam Bake. And we need to ask for extra rolls and coleslaw."

With a quizzical look, Dax said, "What's so special about those items?"

I clutched my hand over my chest like I was having an attack. "Have you eaten there yet?"

"No, but I'm guessing it should have been at the top of my list?"

Shaking my head, I pulled up the menu on my phone. "Pick out your dinner and I'll call it in. And if this doesn't make you want to become a local, nothing will."

While Dax was scanning the menu on my phone, it rang. He handed it to me. "It's Lily."

"Hey, I got your text. We're getting ready to order dinner from The Clam Bake."

Without saying hi, she said, "Change of plans. Meet me at the grange hall and quick." She disconnected and two things crossed my mind. What the heck happened now and how did she get in the building?

"She's at the grange hall and we need to get over there right away." My gut tightened. Just when things were running smooth, she tossed a wrinkle into the investigation. Again.

Chapter 16
Lily

While Milo and I waited for Gage and Dax, I thought how intuitive my book, *Practical Beginnings*, was. Showing me how to unlock something was simply genius. I had no idea the locks had been changed on the building, but they proved no match for my handy dandy new spell. With the guys minutes away, I flicked my wrist, palms up, and at the same time thought about the lights getting brighter and it happened. Like magic. I chuckled to myself. I was getting a handle on this witch thing after all.

Milo stretched out and rolled to his back. "Not bad."

"Thank you, my dear familiar. And none of this would be possible without your support."

"You sound like you're giving an acceptance speech at some awards banquet." He flipped back over and said, "When the boys in blue arrive, I'm going to head home. But don't forget you promised me a special dinner tonight."

"No worries. I've got you covered, fur baby."

I heard the knob wiggling on the back door and strode into the kitchen to unlock it. I had added a magic spell after

I came in like my book suggested to make sure I didn't get an unwelcome visitor. I murmured under my breath the words to unlock and open the door.

"Lily, what was wrong with the lock? It should have opened with the key."

"Just stuck I guess." If my smile was a bit too smug, Gage didn't react but Dax gave me an odd look, as if he had a question but wasn't about to ask it. I hoped Gage wouldn't mention he had changed the lock since that would be harder to explain with Dax standing next to him. "Come on in and let me show you what I found."

The men came inside and scanned the room. Gage said, "I thought we agreed you wouldn't go places alone when you were clue hunting. Especially to my crime scene which is supposed to be restricted."

"Oh, I'm not. Milo is here." At the mention of his name, he trotted through the kitchen and with a backward glance and a flick of his tail, he was gone. "And now that you're here, he's headed home."

Gage brushed his lips over my cheek. "We talked about you and Milo as the dynamic duo but as a cat he's hardly in a position to help you if you need it."

Popping my hands on my hips, I did my best to hide my annoyance. "Milo is a great companion, and I am perfectly safe when he's around." I gave Gage another pointed look.

He threw up his hands. "I give up." And he kissed my cheek again and whispered, "For now."

"To help derail an argument," Dax interjected, "what did you want to show us?"

I gave him an assessing look. There was something different about him tonight. "Did something happen today, Dax?"

He looked at Gage and said, "No."

"Hmm." I started to leave the kitchen, but they weren't following me. I didn't turn around but called over my shoulder, "Are you coming?"

"Right behind you," Gage said.

I walked into the large room that was still filled with various spooky scenes but with the lights on bright there was no thrill factor. "I started thinking about Victor saying he had to refill the candy bowl and that was why he never saw what happened. But he was lying."

We walked through the maze of scenes until we reached the last one, the vampire's lair. Standing in front of it there was crime scene tape where Malcom had once lay, the rust spot evident.

Gage and Dax stood next to me. Waiting.

"We need to walk through what happened that night based on what Josie and Kevin said, along with Victor's observation and then what the evidence is telling us. In addition to who had access to the hall prior to us opening the doors." I snapped my fingers and said, "Don't forget the skinny clown is skinny."

Gage wasn't laughing as he waited patiently for me to continue. "We know when we created the scene, with Corbin's help, the coffin was sitting on the ground but as we can see there was an extension added and that had to have happened after we closed up for the night. Remember the door was ajar when I got here the next day."

There was a small marker where the fake gun had been found. "I think the prop was stored inside the coffin and brought out when the changes were made, with it barely visible since it didn't need to be staring anyone in the face until the police knew it was murder. The scene would be gone over with a fine-tooth comb."

Gage nodded. "All the same conclusions we came to."

"What if Victor and the skinny clown were working together? If they had practiced how they would handle things once Malcom got here. Skinny clown was always meant to be the shooter."

Dax said, "This makes sense but there are bigger questions, like how was Victor involved and who is the skinny clown?"

"Patience, my new friend." I crossed the small space and gestured to the curtain. "No other scene used a curtain to store anything. Victor is the only one who said he had to refill a candy bowl as it was half-empty and went behind the curtain to do it. Dax, were you running out of candy?"

He thought for a minute and shook his head. "Now that you bring that up, no. Very few kids were taking any treats. I overheard the parents were talking about going trick-or-treating after. I can't see how the kids would have been allowed to dip into Victor's bowl any more than the others and we all had the same stuff."

"Exactly my point. Who do we know is in real estate and who purchased their home from Teddy Roberts?"

Gage stuck his hands into his front pockets. "We vetted Victor and he comes up squeaky clean."

I held up my hand to keep Gage from extolling the virtues of Victor. "We heard his mother, Vonni, say how Victor wanted to make his own mark on the world. What if he wasn't measuring up to his father's legacy? He could have been putting pressure on himself to do something his father had never done, take over a community and change the entire vibe. Let's face it, our town is quaint with a bed and breakfast, some excellent but low-key restaurants, and a thriving fishing community."

Gage filled in a few more tidbits, "And our tourists

come in the summer months to enjoy the Maine lifestyle, renting cabins and going on fishing and lobster boats."

"Maybe Victor is planning on having late-night take-out?" Dax shot a smirk at Gage.

When neither man elaborated after I glared at them both, I asked, "Am I missing something?"

"Forget it," Dax said. "If you're on the right track, then who is his partner in crime?"

"I thought you'd never ask." A smile spread over my face. "Corbin Marks."

I thought Gage's jaw was going to hit the floor. "Mild-mannered Corbin? You are joking?"

Shaking my head, I said, "It all fits. First, he's skinny."

Dax snorted. "As am I but I'm not the clown."

A heavy sigh escaped me. "Obviously. You were the fortune teller; besides, you're one of the good guys."

"Gage, don't you remember that Victor told us Corbin was his handyman and then Corbin is the one who builds the scenes for us. He knows how to get in and out of here easily. He also would have known about the hidey-hole under the kitchen sink and because he's so quiet and everyone knows him, no one would have ever guessed it was him."

"What is his motive?" Dax asked but this time the curious tone of his voice captured my attention.

I launched into my working theory. "The oldest one in the book. Money. Working with Victor he must have been impressed by the cars. The house is dripping with all things expensive. Look at his clothes and when he talks about the work he's had done to the place, it screams gobs of money. Corbin has worked hard his entire life in our little town and what does he have to show for it? A work truck and a small house outside of town that isn't fancy. He's a lonely, single guy so having a nice car and money in the bank would potentially attract a life partner."

Gage frowned. Dang, he just didn't want to look outside his comfort zone of suspects. "Then who do you think had motive, understanding the layout, the opportunity, and body size to have pulled off something like this, and remember after the fact they would have to blend into the families to get out undetected."

Dax walked around, looking at the layout with renewed interest. "Gage, she might be onto something. I think we need to take a good long look at Corbin Marks. He ticks all the boxes."

Throwing up his hands, Gage drummed his fist into the palm of his other hand. "He's not a killer. He's just a nice guy who works for anyone who will pay him, and Lily, what's wrong with him living a simple life? He's always struck me as a happy guy."

"Working for Victor showed him how he could live and with the right added incentive that he could do the work on the properties Victor bought plus maybe other bonuses. That might be hard for him to turn down."

"Alright, if I agree to check him out and Dax can do the same on his side of the law, will you promise to not approach Corbin about this theory of yours?" He cocked his head and looked straight into my eyes. "And that means by yourself, with Milo, or another human being. You must stay away from him. Do I make myself perfectly clear?"

I knew I was beaming. "Crystal." I gave Dax a sly wink. "Just like your crystal ball."

. . .

An hour later Gage knocked on my back door and opened it, carrying a box filled with bags with The Clam Bake logo and Dax was right behind him with another box.

"I thought you'd never get here. Did Mr. Wickshire send you out to catch our dinner?" I took the box from Dax and placed it on the counter while Gage did the same. He washed and dried his hands and then opened the cupboard for plates and cups.

Milo slunk into the kitchen and looked at the counter and said, "I thought it was chicken livers tonight."

Dax's eyebrow cocked as Milo meowed at Gage's feet. He looked down. "Don't worry, I had Fred include something for you since you were a good boy and looked out for Lily today."

Milo looked at me. "It's too bad Detective Cutie doesn't actually understand me. I could tell him I wanted liver."

Dax snickered and Milo glared at him. "What are you laughing about?"

Wiping his eyes, he laughed, and I wondered if Dax could understand my familiar. But it wasn't possible.

"Gage, I'll fix Milo's dinner."

He handed me a white box and inside was a plain piece of broiled fish, sans the butter and herbs.

I chopped it up and put half in a clean bowl. "Here you go."

"Great, you're eating scallops or lobster and I'm eating run of the mill fish. That is boring city. How about you slip me something from your plate."

Ignoring him, I helped finish getting everything on the table. "What took you so long? Was The Clam Bake busy tonight?"

Gage sat next to me. "We stopped at the police station and got a few things started regarding our latest suspect. But you should take another look at your clue board since I'm confident you're off base on this one."

Dax scooped up a generous serving of coleslaw and slipped a fried clam down to a waiting Milo. I cocked a brow and he did a one-shouldered shrug. "The poor guy could use some variety."

Milo bumped up against my leg. "I like this guy. Maybe you should have kept dating him instead of Detective Cutie. I could make up a code name for him if you'd like?"

Running my hand down Milo's back, I gently tugged his tail. "You, behave."

I flashed Dax a sweet smile as Milo said, "I'm sure there is a rule in the familiar handbook that goes against pulling my tail."

Popping a piece of dinner roll in his mouth, Dax looked at Gage who was digging in to his dinner, ignoring my conversation with Milo. Heck, I would too if I didn't understand a word he was saying.

Anxious to get back to the topic of suspects, I got up and pulled the clue board out and positioned it so it was in plain sight while we enjoyed our dinner. I popped a fried clam in my mouth and enjoyed the sweetness of the seafood. I couldn't blame Victor for wanting to conquer Pembroke Cove with food this good all year-round.

"We know the clown did it. And I'm sure the clown is Corbin." I held up my hand as Gage sent me a sour look.

"Oh, stop looking like you just ate a pickle. Who else in town has the woodworking skills needed to modify the coffin and is super skinny?" I ate another forkful of coleslaw. "Tucker would know. I can swing by his store tomorrow before I open the shop and see what he thinks."

"You promised no more clue hunting on your own." Gage's tone of voice held a distinct warning to it.

"Talking to Tucker is hardly putting myself in grave danger. It's Tucker and he's a good friend. And he is the only one tapped into the handyman people in town."

Dax said, "I'll go with her, Gage, if that will ease your mind."

Frowning at them both, I said, "I'm perfectly capable of talking to Tucker for a couple of minutes and if I discover anything, I promise to call you right away." I tipped my head and looked at Gage, giving him the same look that had worked before he knew I was a witch.

A small smile tugged at the corners of his mouth. "You are only talking to Tucker and you won't go off tracking down Corbin or anyone else who might be a potential suspect?"

"Correct. And if I get the urge, I'll take someone with me and it won't be Milo." I wouldn't remind him in front of Dax about my newly acquired skills or talk about the fact that now, I could effectively pick a lock. That definitely wasn't a good idea.

Chapter 17
Lily

Once my feet hit the floor the next morning, I had a strong hunch we were running out of time. If Gage and Dax didn't arrest someone in the fraud case before the haunted house ended, the killer might get away. And I for one didn't want Corbin around anyone he might hurt. If he and Victor were in cahoots, it was time to close the coffin permanently on their enterprise in Pembroke Cove.

"Milo, are you coming to the store with me today? I'm leaving shortly so I can swing by Tucker's and ask a few questions about who in town is handy with woodworking tools."

My familiar climbed out from under the spare blanket at the bottom of my bed. He yawned. "Good morning to you too." He did a full body stretch and rolled onto his back, giving me an expectant look like I knew what to do next.

Obliging, I sat down and scratched his belly until he purred with pure delight. The sound was music to my ears and soothing to my thoughts. "You know, just thinking out loud here, but who else might be a good candidate to use tools?"

"Anybody." Milo opened one eye and said, "Except you. Patience is needed to do household projects and the only thing you have patience for are clues. Remember when your front window got broken a few months back and Nate said he'd fix it?"

"Yes, but how is that impatient? It was a broken window." I paused mid scratch.

"You wanted a new window and not just the wood to cover the hole so poor Nate drove downstate to get it for you and install it." He gave me a knowing look. "Patience, zip."

"I'll give you that one. But would you have ever guessed Corbin is the bad guy?"

"What's that saying, it's always the quiet ones?" He flipped over and hopped off the bed. "And I'll hitch a ride to the store. You do what you do best and I will too." He slunk out of the room.

Under my breath, I said, "Snooze in the window."

A low kitty rumble came from down the hall. "I heard that, Ms. Witch."

The sky was a deep blue and the sun was sitting behind scattered clouds, not a bad day for early November and so far, the weatherman had been right. Hopefully, we'd pull out one more day like this for tomorrow. I parked my Mini Cooper behind the store and Milo hopped out and ran through his kitty door. I unlocked the back door, put my lunch in the small refrigerator, and was going to start the coffee pot when I changed my mind. A treat from The Sweet Spot would be perfect and I was headed to the hardware store so it just made sense. I locked the back door and went out the front, calling to Milo in the window seat that I would be back.

Making a beeline across the town park, Tucker's looked to be bustling with people hanging around inside. I needed to approach this like I was looking to hire someone to help out with a few projects. If Nate got wind of it, since he was my usual handyman, I hoped he'd figure out what I was up to. If not, I'd have some apologizing to do.

"Good morning, everyone." I smiled as I entered the store.

Tucker was behind the counter. Mike Shaw was nursing a cup of coffee from a mug with the hardware store logo. Nate was pouring himself a cup so I guessed he turned the lobster boat over to his first mate today, and Dax was smiling at me from the battery display.

"Morning, Lily. What can I do for you?" Tucker said.

I crossed the room and bussed Nate's cheek, hoping he'd just roll with me. "Well, as you know Nate is my favorite handyman in all the world. But since he and Aunt Mimi tied the knot and with his fishing schedule and looking to slow down to semiretirement, I hate to bother him all the time for odd jobs. I was wondering if you could tell me who around town does what kind of work?" Nate didn't react at all as I slid my arm through his, giving it a small squeeze.

Mike chuckled. "Nate, she's saying you're an old goat."

"No." He gave me a wink. "What Lily is saying is that she wants to spread some work around which is good for everyone. I'll always be her main go-to handyman, but there are some jobs that are suited for a person with more time."

Bless Nate. He could read me like an open book. "Tucker, can you give me some referrals? I think most people would stop by here to purchase supplies."

"True. But it all depends on what you're looking to have done."

How was I going to pry information out of him? Before I could think of a new tactic, he said, "Now if you're looking to have a small cabinet or furniture repaired, I'd suggest you talk to Kevin Valentine. He oftentimes has to make repairs for items in his store and has a small woodworking area in his basement."

That was interesting. I had no idea he had skills in that area.

"Then of course, there's always Corbin Marks. The only thing he won't do is build an entire house, but he can do kitchens or replace a faucet. Very talented man and excellent workmanship."

That was high praise from Tucker and I glanced at Mike who was nodding. He said, "Corbin did some work for me last year and I would recommend him in a heartbeat."

The door opened and Gretchen came in. She was dressed casually in jeans, a long-sleeve shirt, and a puffer vest. Giving us a warm smile, she looked at Tucker and said, "I need some lumber. Is it okay if I cut it down in the back to my dimensions so it will fit in my car?"

"Help yourself. You know how to operate the saws, but shout if you need something."

"Thanks, Tuck." She walked to the opposite end of the store and disappeared.

I was dying to ask questions, but it would sound like I was overly curious, which of course I was.

Dax came to the counter with a package of batteries and set them down. "Lily, looks like there's another handy person in town you could talk to." He pointed to where Gretchen had disappeared.

Tucker proceeded to ring up Dax's order. "Gretchen helps out her real estate clients with minor repairs and she doesn't charge them. She figures it helps with higher sales prices, so she'll get more in her commission. Brilliant idea and it helps the sellers too. If the job is too big, she'll recommend they hire Corbin. It's one of the reasons her reputation is what it is."

Without looking at any one person, I said, "A full service agent. That's rare in this day and age." Now this was interesting news. I had three solid leads for people in town who were capable of changing the height of the coffin and all three had access to the grange hall since it was no secret the original lock had many keys floating around town. The next idea came as a sharp reminder; Teddy Roberts had a master key to some of the original buildings in town when they were built and owned by the same person. Could that old master also open the grange hall and would Gretchen have had access to it too?

Dax said, "Thanks for the batteries." He gave me a sly wink. Turned out he was a good partner in my efforts and unlike Gage, he blended in so it made it easy to get what I needed.

I flashed a bright smile to the men and said, "Thanks for your help and Nate, before you go home, can you stop at the store? Aunt Mimi left a book behind yesterday."

He said, "Sure thing."

I went out and turned left to get a coffee and with any luck a cinnamon pecan roll if William had made any today. With my head spinning with possible new suspects, I ran smack into Dax. He grabbed my arms to steady me.

"Were you waiting for me?" I took a step back.

"Are you kidding? With the information you got in

there, which by the way your approach was genius, I had to talk to you." His smile widened. "Headed for coffee?"

"I am and you can buy me a cup if you're going to pump me for information." I adjusted my shoulder bag and stuck my hands in my pockets. Dax fell in step beside me but he didn't pepper me with questions.

When we reached The Sweet Spot, he opened the door and I stepped inside. The aroma of yeasty dough, cinnamon, and coffee greeted me. My mouth began to water since those were telltale signs my favorite treat was in the case.

"Hello, Lily." William came out from the kitchen, his white apron dusted with flour and smears of chocolate and what looked like red berry sauce.

"William, you remember Dax?" I poked him in the arm.

Dax said, "It's nice to see you again. Lily raves about your bakery all the time."

William beamed at the compliment. "I haven't seen you in a week or so, not since before the incident."

"We've been busy trying to get the event relocated. I didn't want us to lose the fundraising night and so many people have volunteered to make it happen at the Stone farm. We're using the corn maze as the backdrop."

"That's an excellent idea." He wiggled his eyebrows. "Are you in the mood for your favorite today? I just finished icing them; they're fresh from the oven."

"Make it two, to go. Dax and I are going back to the shop."

I stepped over to the coffee station and Dax followed me so I handed him a cup. "One of the perks of small-town living. We have the best bakery and the owner knows most everyone's favorites. There's always something special in the case."

"I'm going to have to increase the time I spend on my morning run if I keep eating like this. Last night fried fish and rolls and now bakery items."

Flashing him my best *oh, please look*, I said, "You could use a couple of pounds. If you're here this winter, one gust from a nor'easter will knock you over."

"I'm tougher than I look, ma'am."

I couldn't help but laugh by the serious expression on his face and his imitation of John Wayne—well, at least I thought that's who he was trying to sound like. I withdrew my wallet from my bag.

Dax put his hand out to stop me. "Oh no, I said I was buying today. After all, I'm going to pick your brain when we get back to the bookstore."

I put my wallet away and picked up the white pastry bag from the counter. "William, who would you recommend for handyman work?"

"Corbin Marks for most things, but I had an old rocking chair that had gotten wobbly, and Kevin Valentine fixed it up for me. Did a nice job and reasonably priced too."

It was the same response as Tucker had said. "No one else then?"

"Not in Pembroke Cove. There might be someone good in Pine Valley. Tucker would know. But why isn't Nate helping you out?"

Dax said, "I'm thinking of relocating and I'm all thumbs when it comes to fixing things around the house. I mentioned it to Lily and she said she'd ask around for me."

"Well, I hope you do make the move up here from wherever you live. No place better as far as I'm concerned."

"Thanks for the tip. I'm still in the early thinking stages, but I do like it here. Everyone has been friendly."

He gave me a quick look and I felt my face melt into a

smile. He really was a good guy and if Gage hadn't been in my life, things might have been different. And if he decided to hang around, I'd introduce him to all my friends and we'd help him acclimate.

"I need to get back to my store; it's almost time to open. Thanks for the rolls and coffee, William."

"I'm here every day." He grinned and waved as we left. "Maybe I'll see you tomorrow."

Laughing, we closed the door. Dax said, "He's a great guy."

"Better still, he confirmed what Tucker said about Kevin and Corbin." I glanced around as we crossed the grass, hurrying as the wind kicked up. I noticed Kevin was setting out his open sign for the antique shop. I nudged Dax. "Would you consider him skinny?"

"No, and how could he have been the clown, when he was standing next to his daughter as Sloane hit the floor?"

"True but he could be involved. He has a lot of financial pressure on his shoulders being a single dad and running a business."

"That doesn't mean he's going to resort to crime."

Kevin lifted his arm and waved to us.

I returned the gesture. "All I'm saying is I need to relook at everything and everyone. There is something I'm missing and I can't put my finger on it."

I withdrew the key from my pocket and held it up for Dax. "We need to find out if the town's master key fits the grange hall lock and if Gretchen had access to it."

Dax did a double take. "What do you mean, the town's master key?"

My brow arched. "Surprise. Small towns, all the buildings were originally built by one man and most of us never changed the locks since we didn't know. Until it was discovered that Teddy Roberts had a key and he used it to go into my store while we were looking into Flora Gray's death. If there was one master at his company, who's to say Gretchen doesn't have one too."

"Wouldn't someone have asked that at the time?" He took the key from my hand. "And why haven't you changed the locks?"

"Those are very good questions. First, I'll check with Gage as soon as we get inside, and second, we changed a few things so the master will no longer work." I didn't elaborate that I had cast a spell to protect my store as I unlocked the door and opened it. Milo's head snapped up and he glanced at Dax before settling back into his snooze mode.

"Good watch cat," Dax said.

I gave him a sharp look. "You have no idea." I handed him the bag. "I'll be right back."

After hanging up my jacket and bag in the back room, I called Gage.

"Lily, good morning. Did you sleep well?"

I made small talk in hyper mode and then cut to the chase. "Do you know if Gretchen has a master key to the town buildings and also, would that same key fit the grange hall lock?"

Chapter 18
Gage

Why on earth hadn't I thought of the master key before now? The minute Lily peppered me with her questions, I realized it was a major miss on my part. "I honestly don't know the answer to either question. But I can find out. Are you at the store now?"

"Yes, Dax and I just got back from the hardware store and The Sweet Spot. We're having coffee. Swing by if you want. I'll share my cinnamon bun with you."

Pleasantly surprised to hear they were together, I guessed Dax had figured Lily would get to Tucker's bright and early to ask questions about Corbin, but I was pleased she hadn't gone off on her own. "You enjoy your treat. I'm going to run over to Gretchen's office and ask her about the key. If she has it, I'll take it and see if it fits the old lock. And before you ask, yes, I will let you know what I find out."

She laughed. "How did you know that was going to be my next question?"

"Years of banter."

"You really are the best. Oh, and Gretchen might not be in the office. She was at the hardware store and bought some supplies. Seems she had a woodworking project this morning."

Lily disconnected and I leaned back in my chair. I would like to have been around when she questioned Tucker and I made a mental note to ask Dax how she pulled it off. And the information about Gretchen's actions this morning was interesting. She was a handywoman. Could that mean she was able to rig the coffin? Another thread to pull in the investigation.

Sometimes the best way to get information was the surprise attack approach. Before I left the station, I stopped at the desk. "Lou, any idea where Peabody and Mac are patrolling this morning?"

"They just got in." He pointed to the break room.

"Thanks." The only way to find out what was happening was to go see them. I stepped into the room and said, "Hey, what's going on?"

"There was a break-in at Victor Seidel's place. It doesn't look like anything was stolen and whoever it was only got as far as the garage, but we're going to fill out the paperwork and then get back out there."

"Kids?"

Peabody said, "More than likely. From what Victor said, his office is locked when he's not home and he has a safe on the property so anything of real value was in there."

"What about his mother? Does she have any valuables like jewelry? Maybe someone saw a precious necklace or bracelet when she's been in town and thought that it would be quick to lift it."

"We spoke with Mrs. Seidel and she assured us that nothing was accessible. I'm not sure what that means exactly. She didn't say if she put items in the safe too."

"The woman is a little cagey. Lily and I went out to talk

to Victor a couple of days ago and we had the pleasure of meeting his mother. She wasn't genuinely friendly, just the surface kind of polite."

Mac nodded. "She's the opposite of her son. Victor gave us full access to every room, answered all our questions, and he was relieved when we didn't find anything else out of the ordinary."

"I assume he has cameras everywhere."

"That's where it's odd," Peabody said. "He has an alarm system but no cameras. Claims he doesn't want to feel like he's still living in a city. Figures in Pembroke Cove things are less hostile. And that is his word, not mine."

"Trusting man." With more people getting in-home security cameras, and at least having them cover the main entrances, it seemed odd. For someone who has a lot to lose, he was relying on an alarm to scare an intruder away but no real evidence to charge anyone. "Think he'll change his mind now?"

Mac smiled. "He will if his mother has anything to say about it. She seemed annoyed that he didn't have cameras anywhere on his property."

Now that seemed like the Vonni I had met, pushing her adult son to do as she thought was best. "What was his response?"

Peabody laughed this time. "He assured her that he would give it careful thought. But then he winked at me on the sly. I get the distinct impression he knows how to pacify her and get away with it."

"Anything else happen up there? I'm on my way to Wilson Real Estate."

"Other than Mrs. Seidel said she was going back to Boston tomorrow, not a thing."

"She'll miss her son portraying a vampire and scaring the locals." I tapped the doorjamb and said, "I'll catch up with you later."

Gretchen Wilson's SUV was parked in front of her office. She had a small area set up separate from her home for clients. I knocked on the door before opening it. Even with the welcome sign, I didn't want to startle her.

This was my first time inside and it was well laid out. On one side of the room there was a large window with a view of the backyard behind a desk and a computer. On the opposite side from the door was a leather sofa, a couple of side chairs and a low, round table in the center of the seating area. I thought it was a pleasant way to talk to someone about a future home as this certainly had a welcoming vibe.

Standing behind her desk, Gretchen gave me a warm smile, nothing like the nervous woman from the police station last night, but she was in her element. "Detective Erikson, this is a nice surprise. Are you here on personal or police business?"

"Police."

Stepping out from behind the desk, she gestured to the upholstered chairs. "Why don't we sit here and talk."

I waited for her to take a seat before me. "Sorry to just pop in. This won't take long."

"As I mentioned before, I'm slow until after the new year." She brushed some sawdust from her jeans. "I was working on a project earlier. I need some new bookshelves and it's just as easy to build them myself."

"That's a money saver and it must give you great satisfaction to know when you're finished that you took some flat boards and created a piece of furniture that will last for years to come."

She leaned back in her chair and folded her hands in her lap. "My dad thought I should be as independent as possible so he taught me how to use and respect tools. It comes in handy in work too. I've been known to fix a few things for a homeowner after I take on a listing. Especially some of the older folks on a fixed income. They'll sell their house at a higher price and it's a win for both of us."

I smiled, hoping I looked casual. "Which means you make a larger commission."

"That is true but not everything I do is to fatten my bank account. Which is why I told you about that phone call."

Her tone of voice hadn't changed which indicated she was being honest or she was a consummate liar. "It's refreshing to hear there are still good people in our community. We've had some bumps in recent months."

With a rueful smile, she nodded. "I hope this is the last of the unpleasantness for a long, long time. But I'm sure you didn't come to talk about what has happened in the distant past. How can I help you today?"

"You may not be aware, but when Lily went to the grange hall the afternoon of the haunted house, the door was open. She checked around inside and everything was fine so she didn't think much of it. Maybe the door hadn't been fully latched when we left. You know how these old locks can be."

Nodding, she said, "I double-check every time I leave a showing to make sure all the doors are secured, so I understand. But are you now having second thoughts?"

I said, "When I was investigating Flora Gray's untimely demise, I learned that Teddy Roberts had an ancient master key to some of the buildings in town."

She crossed her arms over her midsection and shook her

head. "Let me guess, he was using it to let himself into buildings around town."

Gretchen was sharp or she had done the same. "I'm not sure how many buildings he accessed other than Lily's. It was then Mimi Michaels confirmed the existence of a master key, but she never felt the need to change the lock since no one had ever bothered her store and she thought it had been lost years before."

"That makes sense. Those buildings have changed hands a couple of times at least and no one would have ever thought there was a master." She tipped her head and gave me a thoughtful look. "Why bring this up now?"

I placed my hands palms down on my knees and leaned forward. "Do you know of another master or perhaps extra keys hanging around for the grange?"

Her eyes widened as the implication hit home. "Gosh, no. I never even knew Teddy had a key. I had heard rumors once it existed, but that was as far as it went. Regarding the grange, there must be twenty keys out there. It is not a secured building. Every time a group asks to use it, Corbin gives them a key."

Sitting up straight, I said, "Corbin Marks?"

"Yes, didn't you know? He's the official custodian of the building. After every function, he makes sure it's clean and all is put back as it should be. He's been doing that for the last ten years at least."

"Thank you for the details, it's important information." I got up and she walked me to the door.

"Detective, I'm not sure what you're thinking, but Corbin is a good person and he'd never hurt a fly."

"I appreciate your input and do me a favor, don't tell anyone about this conversation."

She grinned. "Not even Lily?"

I couldn't help but chuckle. "Whose idea do you think this was?"

Back in my office a half hour later, I pulled up the data we had unearthed regarding Corbin Marks. The office Dax had been using was empty when I walked by and I was curious to know if he had learned anything more. Maybe he was still at the bookstore with Lily.

My stomach grumbled and I picked up the phone to call my mom. She was always good to bounce things off of and I might even wrangle a meal. When she answered, I said, "Hey, Mom, what's for lunch today?"

"Gage, do you only call me during the week when you're hungry?" She tried to sound annoyed, but her words were laced with laughter. "However, in answer to your question, I have a nice chowder simmering and I was planning on making biscuits. Would you like to join your dad and me?"

"Yes, please, and I'd like your opinion on my case if you don't mind."

She said to come over and as she hung up, I heard her say, "Gage is coming for lunch so set another place."

Just as I was picking up my keys from the desk, Lily burst into my office. "Well, hello there." Her face was bright red and she was out of breath.

"Hi," she was able to get out between pants.

"What's the rush? Is there a fire or something?"

"I. Just. Had." Each word was separated by a gulp of air.

I steered her to a chair and gave her a bottle of water from my little fridge. "Take two minutes, then you can talk."

She began to breathe normally and said, "I need to start exercising more."

Perched on the edge of my desk, I chuckled. "That's something we can work on together if you'd like. I run most mornings."

Wrinkling her nose, she groaned. "No." She waved her hand to push that conversation to the back burner. "I was going over my bank statement just a few minutes ago, and I was going to put it through the shredder when I was done. But not everyone does that."

"It's good practice but why did you need to race over here?"

Her face brightened. "It's garbage day and people put out their trash and recycling."

I moved my head in a circular motion, still not sure where she was going with this conversation. "They collect the garbage every week."

She hit the desktop. "Bank statement, garbage day, Corbin. Now did you connect the dots? And I know for a fact he's at the farm working on the scenes."

Then it dawned on me. Trash at the end of the street for pickup was fair game and if Corbin tossed his bank statements without shredding them, I might have a glimpse into his finances.

"Lily, that's a great idea. I'm going to my mom's so I'll swing by and check out his recycling bins."

"No worries. Dax was with me and he's already headed over there, but I thought you would want to meet him." She got up and pushed me off the desk. "You need to go now and don't forget if you don't find anything in the paper bin, he might have tossed it into the regular trash bucket so check both places. But you have to hurry before pickup is finished."

I gave her a side-glance. "Why didn't you go with Dax?"

"I can't close my store on every whim. Besides"—she shrugged—"I tried to reach Aunt Mimi and Nikki but they didn't answer and time was of the essence so I convinced Dax to go, with the promise he would tell me what he found."

I gave her a quick kiss on the cheek and called over my shoulder, "We'll talk later."

I heard her yell back, "Count on it."

By the time I got to Corbin's house, I saw Dax was in a slightly heated conversation with Burke, the garbage man.

"I'm investigating a crime and I need to look through the papers."

Parking across the street, I jogged over. "Burke. What's going on here?"

"This man is trying to rifle through the garbage, and I have a schedule to keep."

I glanced at my shiny truck and knew there was only one way to get what we needed. "What if I took the papers and bagged garbage from the can and you could take cans and bottles?"

He cocked his head and narrowed his eyes. "So, he's on the up and up?"

"Yes, this is Dax Peters and he's a federal investigator working with the Pembroke Cove police on a couple of cases. We have reason to believe there could be important evidence in this trash."

Burke let out a guffaw. "In Corbin Marks' trash?" He opened the lid on the can and pulled out two tied white bags. "Have at it but you gotta promise you won't tell anyone that I let you take it. If there is trouble, I want to steer clear of anything and everything."

That solved my concern of him telling people what we

were up to. I stuck out my hand to seal the deal. After we shook, he said, "Take the bags and your friend can take the papers and we can all get back to business."

Dax and I tossed everything in the back of my truck and I looked at his pressed jeans, dark shirt, and leather jacket. "Are you going trash-picking in those clothes?"

Chapter 19
Lily

Perched on the counter in the store, I thought about Gage. He had stopped at my place last night and filled me in on the search of Corbin's trash only to say there were some papers that were interesting but inconclusive to the case. However, he was still checking into a few things. What the heck that meant was they found nothing to tie him back to the fraud case, the modifying of the coffin, and the biggie, poor Malcom Sloane. I was beyond excited for seven o'clock tonight. We'd finally get things rolling. The weatherman was still predicting a cold but clear evening which promised to bring people out by the carload. Nikki was coming to the store around eleven and we were going over the final details for the haunted house.

Milo came slinking through the bookstore and I said, "What's the matter with you?"

He jumped to the counter and sat down, but instead of cleaning his face as usual, he stared at me. "I'm not sure you should go tonight."

"Why ever not? We will finally be able to wrap up the event and move on to the next one."

His tail swished over my clipboard, ruffling the edges of the paper. "You have put yourself in jeopardy three times in the last few months and it all culminated when you were ready to step back and let Gage and the police handle things. Which was just like yesterday when you let Dax and Gage take over the fact-finding mission on Corbin's trash. Next, you'll get some harebrained idea and rush off, only to put your personal safety at risk. Then you'll dig deep and hopefully find the right spell to hold off whatever crazy is after you before it's too late. And I hate to admit it out loud, but you've really grown on me and I don't want anything to happen to you."

I sank to the stool behind me. That was the sweetest thing Milo had ever said to me. "You're worried about me?"

"That's not what I said; did you hear me?"

Nodding, I placed my hand over my heart and blinked away happy tears. "You might not have said those exact words, but the sentiment was there."

"Whatever. So does this mean you'll stay home tonight?"

I rubbed his head and ears. "I'm sorry but this is my event and I have to be there. But don't worry, I will be perfectly safe and I know a lot more spells than the last time I found myself in a jam. Besides, I thought you said I was becoming a great witch?"

He started to cough as if he was hacking up a fur ball. "Correction, you're a good witch. There is a long way to go before you're great. Like years." He promptly jumped down from the counter and trotted to the window seat.

"Well, you're a great familiar," I called after him.

"You have nothing to compare me to, but for the record, I'm the best of the best."

"Fur ball." I did think about the Corbin connection and

what Milo said had a ring of truth. I was always getting into something right before the culprit was arrested. But nothing was going to happen tonight. Gage and Dax would be around and my spell casting was so much better now. I pushed aside Milo's concern and opened my book, *Practical Beginnings*. It never hurt to practice a little more and my self-protection spell was at times wobbly at best. Maybe Nikki could give me a few tips when she got here.

N ikki blew in like a minor hurricane, fast but not furious. She was glowing from head to toe. I saved my spreadsheet and closed my laptop.

"Someone is sparkling today. Do you have news?"

She dropped her bags on the floor next to the counter and twirled around. "Steve and I set the date last night and we're getting married on, wait for it, St. Patrick's Day."

I whipped my head around. "But you're not Irish, either of you, and Valentine's Day would have been so romantic."

"It gives us an extra month of planning and we might not be Irish, but we do love to celebrate it. Come on, Lily, we love the theme so what do you say? Are you up for it?"

I jumped up, threw my arms around her, and held her tight. "You can count on me and I even look good in green."

Laughing, she said, "That's the spirit. Once we wrap up Halloween tonight, let's start talking wedding tomorrow."

"You got it." I hugged her again, thrilled that she had been able to compromise with Steve about this very important event.

She rubbed her hands together. "What do we need to work on and how can I help?"

I handed her the checklist. "Take a look and let me know if you think I've missed anything. I want to get out to the farm by five to do one final walk-through before everyone shows up and gets into the spirit of the night. Then the doors will open promptly at seven and it will be over by ten."

"Unless people keep coming and dropping money in the box. I say we don't shut down until we don't have any more paying customers. Let's collect every cent we can for the holiday celebrations. We're always right to the penny and if we have enough to increase our fund, I say we do it."

"Good point." I drummed my fingertips on the cover of my book. "Nik, are you comfortable casting the self-protection spell? I'm struggling a bit with it."

She tipped her head and looked at me. "Our books must be really different. I've never seen it before. Show me and maybe I can help figure out where you're having trouble."

Nikki was one of the smartest people I knew and confident she could help. I flipped open the book to the page I had marked only to discover it was blank. I turned a few more pages and they too were blank. I snapped it shut and went in search of Milo. Had I suddenly lost my magic?

He wasn't in the window seat, and when I went back to his blankets, no Milo. I whirled around and he was sitting on the floor looking at me, almost in the same spot where the book had fallen on my head.

I thrust the book out. A combination of anger, fear, and sadness all mixed together wrapped around me. "Something is wrong. The pages in my book are blank. Did I lose my magic and I'm not a witch anymore?"

"Slow down and tell me exactly what happened."

I sat cross-legged on the floor with the book in my lap. "I've been working so hard, reading and practicing the spells as they appear. I know I'm not a great witch and I make a ton of mistakes and maybe I should read the book more. But Milo, all the words on the pages vanished. How do I make them come back?"

In a gentle voice, he asked, "What were you doing when you saw the pages were blank?"

"Nikki and I were talking about a spell and I asked her if she found it hard to perfect and she said it was one she hadn't seen before. She offered to help me so I opened the book to show her and the page was blank, then I started to flip through the rest of the book and discovered they were all blank. What am I going to do?"

"Take a deep breath and answer me one question, which will answer your question. Whose book is this?" He tapped the cover. "Think before you answer that."

I was confused. What was Milo driving at? "It's my family's book passed to me as the next generation." If I had been a cartoon, a light bulb would be glowing above my head right now. "She can't see the pages because she's not a Michaels."

Milo gave me a half nod. "And if she had seen anything in the book, she wouldn't remember or be able to perform the spell. It's all based on you and what you need when you need it."

I dropped my chin. "Now it makes sense, but how will I master everything in there without support?"

"You have Aunt Mimi and witchcraft is based on you. That means you need to pull from your inner resources. Stop thinking about what you can't do. Negative energy will negate anything you try to learn. So, go back out there and have a cup of tea with Nikki before you head home to get dressed for tonight." His eyes were wide as he looked at me. "If I can assume you're still attending?"

"Wild broomsticks couldn't keep me away." I leaned

forward and rubbed his soft gray fur. "Thank you for being the best familiar a witch could have."

He gave a lazy one-eyed wink. "You've said that before, you know. But it never hurts to hear it again."

On the drive back to my house, I was going to drop Milo off and get changed when I decided to give Gage a call.

"Hi there," I said the minute he answered. "Nikki's filling in at the bookstore so I can get ready and head over to the farm. I'm going to do one last walk-through before the gates open. Want to meet me there?"

"Hello, pretty lady. I wish I could, but Dax and I are driving over to Corbin's. We have some questions for him about some money going into his bank account each month."

"Do tell, please. Since it was my idea for you to rifle through his garbage." I heard him sigh and then a door thud. I assumed he was closing his office door so no one could overhear him talking on the phone.

"I can't share everything, but we are going to ask him where the sizeable monthly deposits are coming from, and I want to know more about his relationship with Victor. Either one of two things will happen tonight."

"You could be arresting Corbin, Victor, or both before you make it out to the farm." I didn't bother to phrase it as a question. I was relieved everything was coming to an end and this time, I wasn't involved. "I'm glad. It will be good for everyone to know Malcom's killer will be held accountable. But which one do you think pulled the trigger? Corbin?"

I could hear Gage drumming his fingers on the desktop. "Gage?"

"I'm here. As much as I hate to admit it, all the evidence at the moment indicates it was Corbin. A clown bumped into Malcom and he was dead before he hit the floor. Kevin was with his daughter in plain view of all the other families. Victor was dressed as a vampire and there is no possible way he could do a quick change or even shoot Malcom from where he was standing. It's impossible. Which leaves Corbin. He's the correct body type; he had the opportunity, and by the looks of his bank account, money was the motive. He has to be in cahoots with Victor."

I pulled into my driveway and shut off the engine. "It's logical but still so hard to believe that someone we've known as a gentle and kind man could let money persuade him to commit a terrible crime."

"I agree but by the time I see you tonight, we'll have people in jail and the event will go off as smooth as satin."

I could hear the door open and Gage said, "Gotta go. Dax is ready to roll but I'll see you in a couple of hours."

"Looking forward to it and be careful."

"Don't worry, I'm with Dax."

It was then I heard faintly, "Hey, Lily. Have fun tonight."

"Tell Dax thank you for me."

"Okay. See you later."

After the line was silent, I sat in my car a little longer and Milo waited patiently while I went over what Gage had told me.

"You know, Milo, I guess it's true, money changes people. It's too bad about Corbin. Victor, I guess I could see because of the kind of business he's in, maybe it's easy to become corrupt, but I would never have guessed it would happen to someone as nice as Corbin Marks."

I pushed open the car door and waited for Milo to hop

out. "I'll open a can of tuna for you before I leave, just because you've been amazing through all of this as usual."

"I'll never turn down tuna." He paused with one foot on the bottom step. "Albacore or chunk light?"

I opened the door and waited for him to come up the stairs. "Only the best for my familiar."

He held his head high as he pranced in. "Looks like it's an albacore kind of night."

Chapter 20
Lily

Finally, I was ready to drive out to Marshall's farm for the haunted house. I dressed in layers under my long purple dress to which I added a black wool cloak for extra warmth. It was basically the same outfit from the first haunted house with the exception of sturdy hiking boots to help me walk around the maze without doing a face-plant. I secured my witch hat to my head with bobby pins and double-checked the look, satisfied I was ready to go. I was looking forward to meeting Gage at the farm, but tonight instead of dressing as a broom, he was going to be on duty. And I couldn't wait to tell him that Nikki and Steve had set a wedding date. St. Patrick's Day was still a head-scratcher but whatever the happy couple wanted was fine with me.

I walked into the kitchen and glanced at my clue board. I had yet to figure out who had taken Malcom's cell phone since no one had access to Malcom's car once it went to the police lot and Gage mentioned there was no sign of the locks being tampered with and the car was empty, except for an old coffee cup and candy bar wrapper. But what if the car hadn't been locked when he parked it to go inside the haunted house. He could have left the cell on the seat thinking no one would bother to go into his car. That idea held merit and one I'd talk to Gage and Dax about later since there was bound to be more evidence they'd need for the lawyers.

My cell pinged with a text and I was surprised to see it was from Victor. *What time will you get to the farm? Having an issue with my scene and need your help.*

Can it wait thirty minutes? I hit send.

No. Can you come now? Was his response.

On the one hand I was happy to see the text from Victor; it must mean that he wasn't involved and Corbin was the main culprit. I wanted to call Gage and let him know I was heading out to the farm a little earlier than planned. I thought to ask if we could have a late dinner afterward; we'd have two cars but that needn't stop us. It wouldn't be the first or last time we had to take separate cars someplace.

Be there in ten. I called Gage but he didn't answer. Maybe he was having trouble with cell service. Instead, I left him a quick voicemail and jotted off a note that I had left early and taped it on the back door just in case he swung by. I double-checked to see if Milo was snoozing in the house but came up empty there too. I decided he must be out carousing with his familiar buddies. I left the kitchen light on for him and an extra helping of his favorite tuna for when he got home.

Darkness had fallen early and clouds covered what should have been a bright sky with stars and a full moon. I wished we had thought to string more lights throughout the maze in areas that could be particularly dark but there would be lights from the farm so hopefully it wouldn't be too bad. I'd hate for anyone to trip while being scared out of their boots. But then again, with a little magic, we'd find a way to light it up.

When I parked my car, I wasn't surprised there weren't more in the lot, it was early. I noticed a Mercedes Benz taking up two spots and surmised that had to be Victor's SUV. The passenger door was ajar and the overhead light in the vehicle was on. Curious, I got out of my car, leaving my bag inside, and walked over, calling his name every few steps.

"Victor?" I called again before I rounded the back side of the vehicle. Air rushed out of my lungs. "Vonni!" I hurried to the older woman's side. "Vonni, can you hear me?"

Her eyes fluttered and she finally opened them. "Lily, is that you? Would you help me up?"

I slipped my arm around her slender body and held her steady while she got to her feet. "What happened?"

"I'm not sure what's going on, but when Victor and I arrived, our handyman, Corbin Marks, met us and demanded Victor go into the maze with him. He was so angry and I have no idea why." The older woman's voice shook with fear. "We have to go after them. I'm afraid he intends to harm my son."

I pulled my phone from the pocket of my clock. "I'll call Gage and we'll get the police out here." And if Corbin was here with Victor, where were Gage and Dax?

She clutched my hand before I could dial. "No. It might be too late. We have to try and find them now."

"Vonni, you've had a terrible fright. You wait here and I'll go."

She stood up and straightened her jacket. "I'll be fine as soon as we find Victor but we have to hurry."

The urgency in her voice pushed aside all thoughts of Gage. He would be here soon anyway, especially when he didn't find the men at their homes and got my voicemail. "Alright. But why would Corbin want to hurt Victor?"

She glanced my way and then took my arm as each of her steps grew steadier. "I'm surprised you haven't figured it out yet. The word around town is you're a puzzle master."

How did she know? She was new in town. "I'm sorry, am I missing something?"

"Corbin killed that reporter, Malcom. The night of the haunted house."

That was not what I had expected her to say. "Why? He's not involved with real estate."

With a snort, Vonni said, "He was bragging to my son that he was the mastermind behind the entire thing. He wanted to scoop up all the prime property in town and wait until the heat died down. Then he was going to sell it for a tidy profit to my son who could in turn build a casino and luxury resort. People love going to a pristine ocean location and Pembroke Cove fulfills that checkbox."

"Corbin has lived here all of his life, why would he want to change his hometown to be something unrecognizable?"

She gave me a smile that seemed more predatory than friendly. "He's a small-town hick, just like you, Lily." She wrenched her arm away and now a handgun was trained on me.

"Vonni, what are you doing? We can't help Victor if you're going to hold me at gunpoint." I knew there was so much more to this story but if she thought I was a simpleton, I was going to roll with it and use it to my advantage.

She waved the gun for me to go deeper into the maze. "March. We don't have a lot of time and I need to finish this and get back to Victor's before anyone knows I was here."

"They'll see Victor's car."

"That's because he's here, a tad under the weather at the moment, but soon enough he'll be wide awake with a raging headache. I have another mode of transportation tucked away so I can slip out of the maze unnoticed just like I did at your last haunted house."

And that was when all the pieces fell into place. "You killed Malcom Sloane?"

"Finally." She clapped her free hand on the other forearm. "Bravo."

The sound was muffled by her coat. How could I get the gun away from her and save myself?

"Stop thinking so hard, you might break something." She jabbed the gun toward me and then pointed to the right side of the maze. "Go that way and you can say goodbye to Corbin before he kills you."

"Corbin wouldn't harm me or anyone for that matter." My heart began to race and a trickle of sweat ran down my spine. So much for being cold tonight. I needed to buy more time and keep her talking.

"That's not what the police will believe when they search his work truck. They'll find Sloane's cell phone, the gun that killed him, and stacks of documents that will support he was behind the entire fraud scheme. I've even taken care of the preliminary conversations between him and my son. Of course, Victor is far too smart to get tangled up with a shady deal." Her gaze drifted away for less than a second. "Which was too bad given what he and I could have accomplished together here like I've done before."

"Do you mean he has walked on the shady side of business before but now has found ethics?"

Vonni's face turned crimson, her words laced with venom. "My son has never done anything illegal. My husband and I decided we'd let our nephews do the dirty work and keep our children out of it entirely. Victor had no idea about his father, and my husband would never have let him join the family business. We encouraged our son to make his own mark on the world." She shrugged. "With a little help from us." She gave me a shove and I nearly landed on the ground as I tripped over the hem of my cloak. "Walk. We don't have much time to finish what has begun."

Should I keep her talking or walk in hopes I'd find a way to use a spell to save not only me but Corbin as well. I took a few steps and pretended to limp.

"What's wrong with you?"

I whipped my head around. "When you pushed me, I twisted my ankle."

"Better than being shot. I wouldn't want another kid to see a body. And this maze has better atmospheric lighting than the hall did. It will be scarier for the ticket holders and better to hide my escape."

That was it, my chance to save both me and Corbin. I wasn't worried about Victor; this lunatic would never hurt her own son. What she had said so far indicated she went to great lengths to protect him.

"Vonni, since you plan on silencing me permanently, can you fill in the few blanks I have?"

"If you keep walking, yes. I'll wrap up the case for you. It's the least I can do."

"What was up with the coffin lid and the hiding space underneath it?"

She smiled as I limped another few steps. "A classic misdirection and that included the fake gun strategically placed." She smiled. "Remember when I told you that Victor wasn't handy at all?"

I nodded.

"But I was raised by a carpenter. I spent years following my father around to various jobs and he taught me everything he knew. I was able to jimmy the lock at the hall after you left for the night, make a few modifications to the bottom of the coffin, and then leave the pen to push you toward Corbin. But you never took the bait and I couldn't understand why."

"No motive. Corbin is a nice person and when we were investigating Teddy's death, he never even came up in conversation as a possible suspect. In looking back at Teddy's records, he never even met with Corbin about anything. So, there was no connection."

"I should have added a creative entry to Corbin's logs when I had the chance, but that doesn't matter. There is enough evidence in his truck to convince everyone of his guilt."

She grabbed my arm as I tried to drift to a natural opening in the cornstalks. "Stay on the path. We're almost there."

My time was running out but I didn't want to escape before I made sure that Corbin was going to be safe. Killing me didn't bode well for his longevity either. "Another question."

With a sneer, she said, "My heavens, you are just full of them, aren't you? Last one."

"How did you slip out of the clown costume and get it stashed in the kitchen without anyone seeing you?"

With a smirk, she nodded. "I had plenty of time to get the lay of the land while I was alone in there. You created so many dark spots in the hall that when I was modifying the coffin I picked one out close by and was able to step in there, slip the costume off, hurry to the kitchen, and put it under the sink before those officers had started CPR. For that I will always be grateful to your trusting nature. Not having a security guard at night was just foolish."

That was not a compliment. "Glad I could be of help."

She gave me an appreciative look. "Sarcasm, very nice. You know, spending this time with you, I think we might have been friends if things had been different. You're good with a quip in stressful situations."

"Well, this qualifies."

She grabbed my arm and tugged me to the back side of Victor's vampire scene. This was like watching a bad movie on repeat. Victor seemed to be sleeping. Corbin looked dazed and sported a bloody lump on his head.

I whirled around. "It was you at Malcom's house. You hit me in the back of the head and then cleaned up his house after tossing it. A man would never have been that meticulous. Did you find what you were looking for?"

"Bravo, Lily. You have finally wrapped up the last detail of our close encounters. As much as I loathed Mr. Sloane, I couldn't bear to have people think he was a slob. Sadly, I didn't find all of what I was searching for, but I had already gotten the laptop from his car and downloaded the information I needed. Then I found the papers on his desk and yes, I cleaned up his house as you were taking an unexpected siesta."

She jabbed the gun in the direction of the corn maze. "Now, let's get this over with. Please step into the field behind us and start walking. I'll even give you a chance to run. But don't worry. I'm an excellent shot and you'll never feel a thing."

She was nuts. Did she think I was going to take a stroll and give her a willing target?

Vonni trained the gun on Victor. "If you don't, I'll give him a flesh wound, shoot you anyway, and poor Corbin here will never see the outside of a prison in his lifetime."

It was now or never. "Before I do, can I have a moment to say a prayer?"

She grimaced. "You want to pray? Well, I guess it is a good idea to meet your maker unburdened. Ten seconds."

Good, that was all I needed. With my palms upturned, I said in a clear voice, "Lights on or lights off. The opposite of what is, is what shall be." I flicked my wrists and the corn maze went dark. I pulled Corbin off the ground, shaking him hard, and yelled, "Run!"

He quickly came to his senses and pushed past me. I grabbed the edge of my cloak and twirled three times, as if I were wrapping myself in Bubble Wrap. I concentrated on being protected from all human objects that could harm me. Next, I had to take the gun from her hand but that was a more difficult proposition. She was waving the darn thing as I twirled. I'm sure she was planning to get a shot off when I stopped.

"Gun of metal, carbon or steel—"

I was interrupted by Dax's voice. "Stop! Hands up!" His words cut through the spell I was weaving.

Gage shouted, "Vonni, drop the gun. It's over."

I slowed and came to a stop when Vonni lifted her arm and aimed the barrel of the gun at my chest. A maniacal look filled her eyes and an evil smile graced her lips.

Everything slowed. Dax's mouth was moving but I couldn't hear what he was saying. I was trying to come up with a way to stop a speeding bullet from entering my body as I felt my protection spell slip. Then something strange happened, I felt a surge of energy surround me. I looked to Gage who was focused on Vonni, and then I saw Dax. He was looking at me and the last words that came from his mouth were, "And so it shall be."

T sat on a hay bale while Aunt Mimi and Nikki created a magical screen to hide the vampire section from the people who had come to be scared on a dare by their friends. The screams of delight that filled the air warmed my chilled heart. Peabody and Mac arrived on the scene and escorted a handcuffed Vonni to the police station and the EMTs transported Corbin and Victor to the emergency room to be checked out.

Dax came over and sat next to me. "I guess you now know my secret."

I glanced over my shoulder at my aunt and best friend. "Guess you know about me too."

"We're just a couple of witches in a small town in Maine." He held out his hand for me to shake. "I'd like to formally introduce myself, Ms. Lily Michaels. I'm Dax Peters from Louisiana and I come from a long line of witches."

"It is very nice to meet you, Dax. How long have you known you were a witch?" I bumped his shoulder with mine.

His soft Southern drawl relaxed me a bit. "My whole life, and you?"

"Oh, it's been four months now. I was a bit stubborn reading our family's history."

"Ah, the book. And you're a stubborn witch." He glanced at Gage. "And you're in love with a non-magical?"

I smiled as I caught Gage's eye and he winked at me. "I

am. But you know, I was thinking, you kind of fit in around here so if you wanted to stay in Pembroke Cove, I'm sure there is room for another witch. Aunt Mimi will welcome you with open arms now that you saved her favorite niece."

"That's very kind of you. But I'll have to think about it."

Gage walked over. "Think about what?"

Dax gave me a wide smile. "Lily just asked me to stay in Pembroke Cove permanently."

I stepped into the circle of Gage's open arms. He held me close to his side and kissed my cheek. "If you're looking for a job, I think we can make that happen, and as an added bonus, you'll fit right in with our eclectic little town."

Dax looked from Gage to me. He gave a nod. "You know I don't need to think about it after all. I'll accept your offer on one condition."

Gage said, "And what's that?"

"I want to be the best man at your wedding." He gave Gage a light punch on the shoulder and nodded at me.

"I haven't asked her yet." Gage's grin slid from one side of his face to the other.

"Sir, I'll leave you to it." Dax walked to where Steve had joined Nikki and Aunt Mimi.

Gage stepped away from me and tipped his head. "What do you say, Lily?"

With a snort, I said, "Is that your idea of a *sweep me off my feet* proposal?"

He dropped to one knee and took my hand. "Lily, I know you are never going to stop following clues and solving puzzles. But there is one puzzle that I need for you to solve right now. I have loved you my whole life and I've been dropping hints and leaving you clues as to how I feel. So now, I'm asking you, since this is the only time your sleuthing skills have failed you, will you do me the honor of marrying me?"

Coughing, I said, "It's a good thing we don't have to rely on you for planting clues when it comes to solving puzzles because it is not your strong suit."

"Does that mean you'll say yes?"

I pulled Gage to his feet and placing my hands on his cold cheeks, I said, "Yes. On one condition."

"Name it." He kissed my lips.

"I'm always going to follow the clues and you'll be there to take care of the bad guys."

He laughed. "We might need for you to read more in your book so that you can protect yourself even better, and I'll agree to your condition. Does that mean what I hope it does?"

Tipping my head back as the clouds parted to reveal the moon and the stars, I shouted for all to hear, "Yes!"

Gage picked me up and twirled me around. "She said yes!"

If you loved Scares & Dares help other readers find this book: **Please leave a review now!**
Are you ready to read more from the Lily and the gang in Pembroke?
Keep reading for a sneak peek at
Holidays & Homicide
A Book Store Cozy Mystery Series
Order Now
Or
Shop at Lucinda Race

Not ready to stop reading yet? If you sign up for my newsletter at www.lucindarace.com/newsletter you will receive an excerpt for Cookies & Capers, the introduction of when Lily met Milo right away as my thank-you gift for choosing to get my newsletter.

Holidays & Homicide Chapter 1

Chapter 1

Lily

Tightly closing the door to my bookstore, I hurried down the brick sidewalk in the direction of the police station. But my destination, The Sweet Spot Bakery. Across the street I could see the holiday decorating committee was busy putting the final touches on the decorations around the ice skating rink. The annual holiday Winter Glow and Glide skating party was from seven to nine tonight. This was the first time Gage and I would be going as a couple. I looked at the glove on my left hand, saw a distinctive bump on my ring finger and sighed. We had been engaged for six weeks and it had been the best time in my life. The snow was blowing and creating drifts in the square, and I didn't want to get pulled into a conversation with the volunteers. The store had been busy with holiday shoppers but I needed a quick pick-me-up, and it was easier to zip down Doenut Drive and past the police station to reach my friend William's bakery. And if my handsome fiancé's car, who was also a detective on the force, was in the parking lot, I'd take a quick detour and see if he wanted to join me for coffee. As I rounded the corner I noticed his parking spot was empty.

Pulling the hood of my wool jacket up and tugging on the laces, I braced myself against the freezing cold. The snow was picture-perfect for the holiday season and about time. I thought about how the first storm historically arrived right after Thanksgiving, but not this year. It was mid-December and this was the first measurable snowfall. A sharp toot of the horn caused me to look up, and I waved to Archie Dane, our mailman. His mail truck glided to a stop beside me.

"Hi, Lily, where are you headed?"

Archie's wide smile always elicited a grin from me as he gave me a friendly wink. "Kinda cold out to be taking a walk." Bright-red wool gloves were a sharp contrast to his blue uniform jacket which was neatly pressed. His short brown hair was partially covered by a blue knit hat with the USPS logo on the front. He looked as if he stepped from a recruiting poster for the post office. Well, except for the red gloves. They were downright practical for this weather.

"It's refreshing and hopefully it will bring people out to skate tonight. I'm not sure if you've heard, but Robin's Cafe is donating hot cider and cocoa, and The Copper Kettle and The Sweet Spot are hosting a cookie corner."

"I'm looking forward to it. I've sharpened my skates and am ready to take a few turns around the ice." He looked at the police station behind us. "Will you and Gage be coming?"

My heart sighed. It was the first year that we'd be skating as an engaged couple after all the years we'd been just best friends. It had taken me almost dying at the hands of some crazy lady, and a few close calls for us to open our eyes and state our true feelings. "We're looking forward to it. I just hope I don't spend more time on my backside than my feet."

He said, "I've been walking around my house to practice wearing them again." A wistful look splashed across his face. "If only I hadn't lost at the state championship, who knows how far I could have gone in the world." Tugging on the front of his jacket, he said, "But then I wouldn't be here making sure the mail arrives on time to my friends and neighbors."

I wanted to offer him sympathy that all works out for the best, but knew that no real words would comfort him. Never having experienced that type of setback, I decided to ease away from the topic. "Are you bringing someone with you tonight?"

The smile was back. "Noelle Webber. I met her a few weeks ago. She's a driver at We DOT Shipping. We met delivering a package to the same place, and then I bumped into her again at the Magical Moonshine Pub in Robin's Pointe—that's where she lives. I think it was fate."

I was genuinely pleased Archie had met a nice girl. At least I was assuming she was since he deserved someone special. "I'm looking forward to meeting her tonight."

Gripping the steering wheel, he said, "I'd better get going. Mail delivery needs to get done so I can get to Robin's Pointe and back in plenty of time to take Noelle for dinner before the Glow and Glide starts. It's her first time skating, and I'm hoping she enjoys it."

"I'm sure she will with you by her side." If I hadn't been paying attention, I wouldn't have noticed the corners of his mouth deepen to a brief frown. "Yes. I need to get my coffee and get back to the store. With Christmas two weeks away, I'm in for a hectic day."

Saying goodbye, Archie tapped the horn one more time as he pulled away. I watched as the small white vehicle took a left turn on Route One, leaving town and not heading where I thought his route went. I did feel bad for whatever was troubling him. The next time I got the chance, I'd ask him, just to make sure there wasn't trouble that I could help him fix. I pulled my collar close to my face and hurried down the sidewalk. Winter in New England had finally arrived.

I was getting ready to lock up my bookstore for the day when the front door opened. Milo, my familiar, sat up on the front counter where I was working and said, "Well, look who's here; it's Detective Cutie."

My fiancé was tall and well built, with the dreamiest hazel eyes and light brown hair. I could see from where I was standing his vintage cherry-red pickup was parked next to the curb. He crossed the room with a swagger full of confidence but not cocky. "Hello." Gage's deep voice warmed my heart. His voice held the same smile that was on his lips. Leaning in, he kissed me.

"Hello, yourself. I thought you were picking me up at home?"

His finger trailed down my cheek and gently pushed my chin up, tilting my face to him. "I couldn't wait another minute to see you."

My heart sighed as this kind of talk could potentially sway me from going skating, but I knew as a shop owner I needed to be at the event to support the town. "I'm glad you did."

Milo started hacking up a hairball. "People can see you through the window." He jumped down, trotted to his window seat, and then hopped up and settled onto the cushions.

Ignoring him and looking past Gage as the darkness fell, I said, "Did you see the tree in the square?"

He glanced over his shoulder. "You mean the lobster traps stacked to resemble a Christmas tree?" He smiled again. "It's hard to miss with all those twinkle lights and shiny baubles."

Now, I sighed loudly. "I think it's a wonderful idea, and it will save a tree, and it's in plain view of my shop so I can look at it until after the New Year."

Cupping my cheek, he grazed my mouth with his. "I think the view inside is much better. Maybe we should stay in tonight."

Laughing, I gave him a little shove. "Why, Detective Erikson, are you trying to divert my attention away from tonight's event?" I knew that was exactly what he was trying to do. The last time there had been a major town event, someone had been killed, and of course, I started investigating. Solving it had been one of my finer moments, but Gage would never agree since I almost became a ghost.

Straightening, he said, "Can't blame a guy for trying."

I shooed him away from the counter. "Let me finish up, and we can go back to my house and have a quick bite of dinner. I want to get to the rink early. Archie Dane is going to introduce us to his new lady love. He said she's from Robin's Pointe."

He wiggled his eyebrows. "I wonder what she's like. Any idea how they met?" He took a chocolate kiss candy from the jar next to the cash register, unwrapped it before handing it to me, and then he took another for himself.

"They were both delivering a package to the same place, and they clicked instantly from what he said." I popped the candy in my mouth, letting it melt on my tongue. I loved the creamy and sweet treat, and Gage indulged with me.

He twirled a finger around my face. "I hope Archie's girl gets the same expression when he gives her a piece of chocolate." He pecked my lips and a flirtatious gleam filled his eyes. "Are you sure we can't skip skating? It's pretty cold out, and it might snow again."

"Gage, you're incorrigible. Now, make yourself useful and either pick up dinner or sit in that wingback chair and wait for me to finish. The more you distract me, the longer this takes."

Holding up his hands in surrender, he said, "Fine, fine. We'll go skating, but you're buying me a cocoa, maybe two."

I arched my brow and gave him a look that said, *really?*

"Or I'll buy." He laughed. Sitting in the chair, he asked, "How was business today?"

"Brisk, and not a single thing out of the ordinary happened." I finished putting the cash in the money bag and slid it into my tote. "Okay, I'm ready. I'll go out the back and meet you at the house."

"Come on. I'll drive you home. The roads are slick and we can pick up your car later."

That was an offer I wasn't going to refuse. My Mini Cooper was great in the snow because it sat low and wide to the ground, but riding with Gage was more appealing. "Milo, are you coming with us?"

"It's better than getting wet paws tramping through the snow." He landed with a soft thud on the floor and waited patiently next to the front door.

I locked up in the back room and grabbed my coat, hat, and mittens. Now I was ready. Going back into the store, I said, "Let's get this party started."

After getting cocoa coupons from Gil Akers, Gage and I glided around the outskirts of the rink, holding hands and grinning like teenagers. The turnout was fantastic; it seemed like most of the town was here. I was surprised to see Chet Harvey at the cookie station, helping William pass out sugar cookies. I waved to Aunt Mimi and her husband Nate, my best friend Nikki and her fiancé Steve, and Ellen Pease and her teenage son, Wyatt. I could see my folks looking more like kids than my parents on the opposite side of the ice, grinning from ear to ear.

I poked Gage in the ribs. "Look, there's Archie with his girl, and he's wearing his Santa hat. How festive!" He casually looked in the direction I had indicated. I held up my hand and gave them a wave. "Come on. Let's skate over and meet her."

Taking the direct route, we made a beeline across the ice to where Archie was helping his girlfriend stand. She seemed to be a little wobbly as her ankles bent in before she straightened them again, showing off the skates with bright red laces, and then promptly sat down on the bench.

"Hello." Puffs of frozen air danced between us. Extending my hand, I said, "I'm Lily Michaels, and this is my fiancé, Gage Erikson."

Archie was beaming. "This is Noelle Webber." He dropped his chin and looked at her with wide eyes. "My girlfriend."

He frowned and I glanced in the direction he was now glaring. Chet Harvey and Gil Akers were in his line of sight, and Ellen was slightly behind them. I had to wonder what that was all about, but I turned to chat with Noelle. She had long brown hair and bright blue eyes, and from her sitting position, she seemed to be taller than me.

"Hi." Her voice had a breathy quality, almost as if she

was shy. "It's a pleasure to meet you. Archie's been talking about tonight since we met. He said I just had to come. It is the highlight of the holiday season and all." When she looked up, her eyes locked on Archie. "So far it's been fun."

He pulled her to a standing position and her ankles bowed in again. He slipped an arm around her waist and said, "Don't worry. I won't let you fall."

Smitten was the word that came to mind and it seemed to be reciprocated. "It was really nice to meet you, Noelle. Enjoy your evening, and don't forget to get a cup of cocoa. Regan, who owns the café, is running the stand and it always hits the spot."

Archie said, "Thanks," as he pushed off, holding her tightly to wind their way around the rink.

Watching them for a minute, I glanced at Gage. "Noelle seems nice but quiet, but I think that will suit Archie." My attention was drawn to Aunt Mimi, who was waving at us to join them. "Come on. I'll let you buy me a cocoa now, and we can see what my aunt is all excited about."

We glided to a stop next to the cocoa stand where Mimi and her husband Nate were. "Hey there." I kissed her cheek. "Are you having a good time?"

Aunt Mimi and I looked very much alike, except she was in her mid-seventies with silver gray hair, but at one time it had been chestnut brown like mine. And you'd never guess her age by her youthful grin and spirit and the mischievous glint in her brown eyes. She was a witch. Now that I knew our family was part of the Pembroke Cove witches, I wondered if that was why she always looked exactly the same She never aged, or maybe it was just good genes.

Nate grinned. "The best time." He glanced at the sky. "The stars are out and our Christmas tree is stunning."

"How many of those lobster traps are yours, Nate?"

He beamed with pride. "A good many, and it was fun building it. Not so much fun when we have to deconstruct, but I'm not going to think about that tonight. Right now, it sets the perfect tone for our little seaside community."

Aunt Mimi said, "I'm having your parents over for brunch next Sunday. Please tell me you'll come. I've already invited Nikki and Steve too and of course Gage's parents. I just love this time of year and we have so much to be thankful for."

I wasn't sure if she was talking about the engagement or the fact that I escaped an untimely death four times in the last six months. Gage asked, "What can we bring?"

"Just yourselves." She gave him a kiss on the cheek. "Now, you two should take another spin around the ice before the night gets too cold."

"Yes, Aunt Mimi." I gave her another kiss and did the same to Nate before taking the insulated cup of cocoa from Regan and slipping my arm through Gage's. Over the next couple of hours, we made our way around the ice. We chatted with my parents, Gage's mom and Dad, and Nikki and Steve. They all confirmed they were going to Mimi's on Sunday. As we made one final turn on the ice, I tipped my head back and looked up at the stars. "It is a perfect night."

Gage glanced at the thinning crowd. "It seemed everyone had a good time."

I took his hand. "It's the holidays. What could go wrong?"

A Free Story for You

Have you enjoyed Scares & Dares? Not ready to stop reading yet? If you sign up for my newsletter at www.lucin darace.com/newsletter you will received Cookies & Capers which is the start of Lily and Milo's adventure as my thank-you gift for choosing to get my newsletter.

Cookies & Capers

I stood in front of the old wood and glass door as I pocketed the keys to the Cozy Nook Bookshop. Aunt Mimi had signed her bookstore over to me. She said it felt like giving me her baby. But I loved the shop as much as my aunt did. We had worked together for the last twelve years. After attending the University of Maine, I had a degree in history and education. I had always wanted to be a teacher, but jobs were scarce and after substituting for a few years, I moved back to my hometown of Pembroke, Maine, and Aunt Mimi hired me as soon as I unpacked my suitcase.

Spending time with my aunt, learning the business, had been the best experience. I offered to buy the shop when she wanted to retire, but she wouldn't hear of it. As long as she had free books for life, and her long-term boyfriend Nate, she said it was a fair deal. From my point of view, I had built-in backup for years to come.

Now that I was the bookshop owner, Aunt Mimi was no longer coming in every day which meant her cat, Phoenix, wasn't either and the space felt empty without a kitty lying in the window or skulking about as kitties do. I was off to the Pembroke Animal Palace to see if I could find a match.

It was a short walk in the bright noonday sun. The spring air from the ocean carried a tang of salt, but the breeze was refreshing. I waved to one of my best friends, Gage Erikson, as he drove past in his police-issued sedan. My heart fluttered in my chest.

He was a detective on the force. Not that we had much crime in our small seaside town. But one of these days I was going to get brave and tell him I had been carrying a torch for him since we were in ninth grade. What's the worst thing that could happen? We'd still be best friends, right?

I continued down the brick sidewalk, waving to William North from the Sweet Spot Bakery. He was sweeping the area around the small bistro tables in front of the bakery. William was wearing a large pristine white apron and a wide smile. A deep inhale confirmed my suspicion. He was baking cookies. My mouth watered. I did a half turn and went back to where he was finishing up. "Good morning, William." I bobbed my head in the shop's direction. "What is that tantalizing smell?"

He held open the brightly polished glass door. "One of your favorites, Lily. Chocolate chip and pecan cookies. Can I interest you in one before you continue on your mission?"

I gave him a side-look. "Mission?"

He chuckled. "Over the years my Lulu had said you

had two speeds, strolling and purposeful. Just now it was purposeful so hence you're on a mission."

"I'm going to the shelter, hoping to find a kitty. The shop is lonely now that Phoenix is home every day with Aunt Mimi, and I think a cat napping in the window adds an air of serenity to the place."

"Unless you're allergic."

He had a point, but I was not willing to be deterred. I smiled. "I'm always happy to deliver to a customer." I leaned over the glass bakery case, like a kid pressing her nose against the candy case. "You made sugar cookies too and frosted them?" I sighed. I was going to need to exercise more if he continued to bake all my favorites. He was smiling at me as I looked up. "Are the chocolate pecan ready?"

He wiggled his eyebrows. "I have a tray cooling in the back."

"Then can I have one of those and a sugar cookie, but to go?"

With a flick of his wrist, he snapped open a white bakery bag and called over his shoulder. "Jerilyn, would you please bring out the last batch of cookies?"

I heard a muffled, coming, and smiled. "It's good that Jerilyn stayed on." I said nothing about his beloved wife Lulu. Rumor had it she was ill and not doing well.

He nodded. "It is. She's a hard worker and excellent with the customers."

Jerilyn bustled in from the back room carrying a large stainless-steel tray. It was lined with parchment paper and cookies the size of the palm of my hand. It was going to taste so good with a hot cup of tea later.

William put two in the bag, along with two sugar cookies, and then he handed it to me. I paid for my cookies and thanked him. "Stop by the shop later. You might just get to meet my new fur baby."

"Sounds like a plan." He grinned and crossed his arms over his rounded midsection. "You're more like your aunt than you realize. Ever since she opened that bookshop, she's had a cat, too."

I paused, tucked the bakery bag in my tote, and with my hand on the door, I turned and gave him a wide grin. "And now it's time I carry on the tradition." With a jaunty wave, I called, "Wish me luck."

Cookies & Capers is only available by signing up for my newsletter – sign up for it here at www.lucindarace.com/newsletter

Love to read?

Cozy Mystery Books
A Bookstore Cozy Mystery Series
<u>Books & Bribes</u>
It was an ordinary day until the book of Practical Magic conked Lily on the head causing her to see stars. And then she discovered her cat, Milo, could talk.

Catnaps & Crimes
The fun continues as Lily practices her magic and needs to investigate another murder.

Tea & Trouble
A fall festival, reading tea leaves and a few clues propel Lily into a new murder investigation.

Love to read?

Scares & Dares
*What goes wrong at a haunted house is anything but
expected until Lily starts following the clues.*

Holidays & Homicide November 2023
Can Lily solve a murder before it ruins the holidays?

Leprechauns & Larceny February 2024
Will a dead leprechaun take the shine off the wedding?

Cowboys of River Junction

Stars Over Montana
*The cowboy broke her heart but he never stopped loving her.
Now she's back ready to run her grandfather's ranch...*

Hiding in Montana
Can love flourish while danger lurks in the shadows?

Moonlight Over Montana
*From the smoldering ash, she realizes he's all the family she
and her daughter need.*

Second Chances in Montana January 2024
*Twenty years later Renee and Hank are back where they fell
in love but reality is like a spring frost. Is a long-distance
relationship their only option for a second chance?*

The Sandy Bay Series
Sundaes on Sunday
*A widowed school teacher and the airline pilot whose little
girl is determined to bring her daddy and the lady from the
ice cream shop together for a second chance at love.*

Love to read?

Last Man Standing/Always a Bridesmaid
<u>Barrett</u>
Has the last man standing finally met his match?

<u>Marie</u> *May 2023*
Career focused city girl discovers small town charm can lead to love.

The Crescent Lake Winery Series
<u>Breathe</u>
Her dream come true may be the end of his...
Crush
The first time they met was fleeting, the second time restarted her heart.
<u>Blush</u>
He's always loved her but he left and now he's back...the question, does she still love him?
<u>Vintage</u>
He's an unexpected distraction, she gets his engine running...
<u>Bouquet</u>
Sweet second chances for a widow and the handsome billionaire...

Holiday Romance
<u>The Sugar Plum Inn</u>
The chef and the restaurant critic are about to come face to face.
Last Chance Beach
<u>Shamrocks are a Girl's Best Friend</u>
Will a bit of Irish luck and a matchmaking uncle give Kelly and Tric a chance to find love?

A Dickens Holiday Romance

Love to read?

<u>Holiday Heart Wishes</u>
Heartfelt wishes and holiday kisses...

<u>Holly Berries and Hockey Pucks</u>
Hockey, holidays, and a slap shot to the heart.

<u>Christmas in July</u>
She's the hometown girl with the hometown advantage.
Right?

<u>A Secret Santa Christmas</u>
Christmas just isn't Holly's thing, but will a family secret
help her find the true meaning of Christmas?

It's Just Coffee Series 2020
<u>The Matchmaker and The Marine</u>
She vowed never to love again. His career in the Marines
crushed his ability to love. Can undeniable chemistry and a
leap of faith overcome their past?

The MacLellan Sisters Trilogy
<u>Old and New</u>
An enchanted heirloom wedding dress and a letter change
three sisters lives forever as they fulfill their
grandmothers last request try on the dress.
<u>Borrowed</u>
He's just a borrowed boyfriend. He might also be her true
love.
<u>Blue</u>
Will an enchanted wedding dress work its magic one more
time?

Love to read?

The Loudon Series

Lost and Found
Love never ends... A widow who talks to her late husband and her handsome single neighbor who has secretly loved her for years.
The Journey Home
Where do you go to heal your heart? You make the journey home...
The Last First Kiss
When life handed Kate lemons, she baked.
Ready to Soar
Kate will fight for love, won't she?
Love in the Looking Glass
Will Ellie's first love be her last or will she become a ghost like her father?
Magic in the Rain
Dani's plan of hiding in plain sight may not have been the best idea.

Social Media

Follow Me on Social Media

Like my Facebook page
Join Lucinda's Heart Racer's Reader Group on Facebook
Twitter @lucindarace
Instagram @lucindaraceauthor
BookBub
Goodreads
Pinterest

About the Author

Award-winning and best-selling author Lucinda Race is a lifelong fan of reading. As a young girl, she spent hours reading novels and getting lost in the fun and hope they represent. While her friends dreamed of becoming doctors and engineers, her dreams were to become a writer—a novelist.

As life twisted and turned, she found herself writing nonfiction but longed to turn to her true passion. After developing the storyline for A McKenna Family Romance, it was time to start living her dream. Her fingers practically fly over computer keys as she weaves stories of mystery and romance.

Lucinda lives with her two little dogs, a miniature long hair dachshund and a shih tzu mix rescue, in the rolling hills of western Massachusetts. When she's not at her day job, she's immersed in her fictional worlds. And if she's not writing romance or cozy mystery novels, she's reading everything she can get her hands on.

Made in the USA
Columbia, SC
07 January 2024

29984161R00120